Dog Spelled Backwards:
An Unholy Mystery

By Jill Yesko

Also by Jill Yesko
Murder in the Dog Park
Sleeping Dogs Don't Lie

Baxter World Publishing
1953 Greenberry Road
Baltimore, MD 21209

www.murderinthedogpark.com

Cover design: Victoria Brzustowicz,
victoriabcreative.com
Author Photo: Jim Burger

ISBN: 978-0-9854852-1-4

Acknowledgements

Dog Spelled Backwards would still be a draft file on my computer if not for the support and editorial guidance of fellow author and artist extraordinaire, Rick Shelly. Heartfelt thanks for seeing me through this process with patience and humor. Thank you Chris Kosmides, John Ross and Lawrence White of the Hampden Writing Group for your unflagging support, friendship and good cheer. Extra special thanks to Linda Lenhoff for never getting tired of me, even when I ranted and rambled; Debbie Janka for keeping me sane in a dog-eat-dog world; and Ginny Tata-Phillips and Melissa Kyle for friendship and basset hound advice.

I encourage you to consider adopting a dog from a rescue organization such as Blue Ridge Bull Terrier Rescue, www.brbtc.com.

A woman of valor, who can find? Far beyond pearls is her value.
Her husband's heart trusts in her and she shall lack no fortune.
She repays his good, but never his harm, all the days of her life.

Proverbs

1 Lenny Gets Religion

I covered my ears to drown out Don's bastardized rendition of "Sweet Home Alabama." At the first sound of Don's off-key singing, Archie buried his head into a pile of dirty laundry.

"Yeah, Don can't sing for shit," I said to Archie, my black and white bull terrier. "Good thing he's got other redeeming qualities."

In a hot second I was peeling off my clothes, about to surprise Don in the shower for a quickie before his shift began. A steamy shower with some morning sex was exactly what I needed to unkink my body after sitting on my ass for ten frigid hours on a fruitless stakeout.

I'd just stripped down to my panties and was about to fling them into the hamper when Lenny pounded on the door. Don may be a Baltimore City police officer, but my cousin Lenny was the unofficial captain of the Baltimore sex police. He had an uncanny knack for showing up just as Don and I were about to get down and dirty. I considered ignoring the knocking. If I didn't let him in, Lenny would continue pounding on the door then hitting the door bell until his finger bled. Sex would have to wait.

I pulled on one of Don's Baltimore Ravens sweat shirts and wriggled into my jeans. I opened the door and flipped Lenny the bird. He breezed by me, unfazed, taking his usual seat on the battered couch. "Here boy," he called out to Archie, who jumped on Lenny and buried his egg-shaped head into Lenny's coat pocket, rooting around for a scrap of food like a pig after a truffle.

"Coffee?" I asked rhetorically, knowing Lenny could easily drink the whole pot of

Dog Spelled Backwards

french roast that I'd just brewed. "Extra cream and sugar, please," he replied.

I poured two cups and handed him a steaming mug. After downing the coffee in a few gulps he was bouncing on his heels and playing with strange-looking long white strings hanging out of his white button down shirt. Archie snapped his powerful jaws at the long strings.

"What's with those strings? You forget to cut the price tags off your clothes?"

"Not funny Jane," Lenny said solemnly. He tapped what looked like a crocheted beanie on his head.

"What's that stupid thing? Did you lose your Oriole's hat?"

"It's my *yarmulka*. Jewish men wear it," Lenny said proudly. "It's a sign of respect to God. And these,"—he fingered the strings—are called *tzitzit*. They are ritual fringes worn to—"

I cut him off. "Nice that you've got yourself a Halloween costume, but I'm late for work. Let's have this Sunday School lesson another time."

"I hear that you and Don are getting married," he said, winking at me.

"Yeah, and the Orioles just won the World's Series for the third year in a row. You got any other hot air you want to blow up my butt this morning?"

"Don's already asked me to be the best man," Lenny said holding out his mug for me to refill it. "I am truly honored."

"Well honor your lazy ass self by getting your own coffee," I snorted. "When and if Don and I get married, I'll be sure to include you on the group email."

Lenny shrugged and got up to fetch another cup of coffee. He sat back down on the couch, took a sip, and folded his hands over his paunchy stomach.

"It's time you heard the truth. That's why I've come today," he pronounced with exaggerated solemnity.

"Enough suspense, your holiness," I mocked, pouring myself a cup of coffee. "What nugget of wisdom do you have to impart?"

Dog Spelled Backwards

"You're Jewish. And so am I."

I rolled my eyes.

"Your mother never told you?"

I squinted at Lenny. Was he pulling my leg? "Why would she tell me a lie? We're Polish Catholic. End of story."

"We're Jewish, Jane, and you are going to have to deal with it, the sooner the better."

"Don't patronize me," I hissed. " Can you prove I'm Jewish?"

Lenny grinned. "Two words: 'St. Wojciech."

How the hell did he know about that place? The only one who knew about what happened to me there was my mother. And she was dead.

Just then, Don walked in from the kitchen dripping wet with a small towel wrapped around this waist. "Hey Lenny! What's up future brother-in-law? You save some coffee for me?"

Don pulled a quart of milk out of the refrigerator, downed it, then put the empty back carton back in. Archie stuck his head in the open refrigerator and trotted away with a loaf of bread in his jaws.

"Drop it, Archie!" I screamed. He hunkered down under the coffee table and ignored me. In a flash, he'd dismantled the loaf and was contentedly chomping down the last bits of pumpernickel.

Don hugged me tightly from behind. "Janey, I'm glad we're having a Jewish wedding. That would make your late mother so happy."

"Hands off, Don," I ordered, breaking free of his bear hug.

"What's all this b.s. about a wedding? Don, have you been drinking? Lenny, you need to mind your own business. Maybe the two of you should get married." Archie whined and thumped his powerful tail.

"Now if you all will excuse me, *someone* around here has work to do."

I grabbed my backpack, put on my leather motorcycle jacket and whistled for Archie. I slammed the front door on the way out. Where did Lenny get these crazy ideas? Yeah, he was my only living relative, but that didn't mean I had to listen to him.

As I backed my ancient Toyota Corolla out of the parking lot, a shiver of doubt ran down my spine. Could there be even a tiny shred of truth to what Lenny had said about me being Jewish? More importantly, was Don serious about getting married?

I had a very bad feeling my new normal life was about to go sideways.

2 Zyd

I accelerated onto the Beltway and lit a cigarette with shaky hands. I took a long, hard drag to steady my nerves. A painful memory that I'd thought I'd pushed to the farthest reaches of my nicotine-addled brain hit me as I sat helplessly in a traffic jam. Lenny's crazy talk bout religion had me rattled like a box of lug nuts on a flat bed. Although I tried never to think much about my childhood, what Lenny said about being Jewish stuck in my craw.

I remembered the Easter Sunday I turned twelve. My mother again forced me to attend mass at St. Wojciech Roman

Catholic Church in Fells Point. The Easter mass was a three hour-long slog in Polish and Latin; an interminable recitation of Christ's passion.

The service began at sunrise, so I had to get up at the ungodly hour of five am. After loading my belly to the bursting point with a Polish peasant breakfast of kielbasa, bacon and farmer cheese, I put on a stiff pinafore dress and ruffled ankle socks—an outfit way too itchy and girlie for my tom boy taste. Then my mother frog marched me to the car. I asked why she didn't go to church. Her answer was always the same. "I have to clean Mrs. Rosenberg's house, my arthritis is acting up..." I knew my mother was lying, but if I confronted her, she'd whack me with her plastic spatula. So I kept my mouth shut and cracked my knuckles as we drove in silence down the Jones Falls Expressway.

At six o' clock, my mother deposited me at St. Wojciech's and squealed away without waving good-by. I stood on the marble steps with a knot in my stomach and sense of dread. It was so cold that I could barely sit still. The church's ancient heating system was on the fritz, and the main chapel was as icy as a meat locker. I stoically sat still in the ass-breaking wooden pews alongside a coven of grumpy Polish women. They spoke English with unintelligible accents and shot me dirty looks in between mumbling their prayers to Jesus and St. Casimir.

I had to pee. As I got up to use the bathroom, Mrs. Goralski, the church's oldest member, grunted and tugged me to the hard seat. I crossed my legs and tried to pray like she did, with the fervor of a true believer. I twisted my rosary beads in my tiny hands and asked God to help my mother earn money so we could pay our bills and move out of our cheap apartment. I prayed that Lenny and I could move into a real house so we could have a lawn and get a dog like my better-off classmates.

Shifting the rosary beads into my other hand, I prayed that my mother would lose her Polish accent and Old World ways so she would look like a normal American

Dog Spelled Backwards

mother, like the mothers on TV reruns of "The Brady Bunch."

I implored God for these blessings. Deep down, I knew that my prayers would not be answered no matter how many times I made signs of the cross or uttered *Zdrowas Marjo*, "Hail Mary" in Polish. Nobody listened to me at St. Wojciech's, not even God.

Maybe God ignored me because I was different from the other people at St. Wojciech's. With my dark hair, wide-set brown eyes and skinny body, I stood out from the sturdily built, blue-eye women. The women next to me in the pews had thick ankles and weightlifter arms, they reminded me of human draft horses. Even my clothes were different from the other parishioners. My simple dresses from second hand shops fit me like a scarecrow on a starvation diet. My shoddy clothes paled next to the intricate embroidery and rich colors of traditional dresses worn by the other women. I felt like an outcast, even more so because my mother never came with me and my father was dead.

During mass, I worked out long division problems in my head and knotted and unknotted my rosary beads while the other parishioners genuflected and prayed their hearts out to the Miraculous Medal Novena Shrine. I shuddered at the Byzantine icons that loomed with expressions of pain and suffering etched into their taut, Eastern European faces. Gazing at the Black Madonna shrine to Our Lady at Czestochowa that sat above the altar, I was sure she was staring down at me angrily. I wanted to stick out my tongue, run out of St. Wojciech's, and never look at her again. I got up to leave, but Mrs. Goralski pushed me back down into the pew with her bony hand and hissed, "Sit down you little *Zyd*."

Only Father Marek was nice to me. With his beak-like nose and bad comb over, he looked like a priestly version of Big Bird. He always said kind words and smiled beatifically when he placed the communion wafer on my tongue. At Easter and Christmas, Father Marek always gave me an extra chocolate bar. "For you to enjoy later," he would say, patting me on the head.

After three droning hours, the Easter mass finally ended. As the parishioners left the pews, they hugged and talked about visiting their families for Easter dinners of ham and *gwumpke*, polish dumplings. But they said nothing to me, giving me only rude looks, even though I was on my best behavior. They didn't even wish me *wesolego alleluia*, the traditional Easter greeting. I wanted to cry, but I held back tears because I didn't want anyone feeling sorry for me. After mass, I stood alone on the church steps like a forgotten parcel.

When my mother's car finally pulled up, I ran down the steps and jumped in. As we drove along, I pulled out my rosary beads, rolled down the window, and threw them onto Broadway. I hoped a truck would crush them.

"Vy you do zat?" my mother scolded in her heavily accented English.

I burst into tears and wailed. "Because everyone but Father Marek hates me!"

She put her hand on my knee. "One day you vill understand."

I looked my mother square in the eye. I'd never challenged her before.

"Why don't you don't go to church?"

She clenched her jaw. "I explain it ven you are older. From now on, you not go to church anymore. You stay vit me on Sundays."

When we arrived home, I ran to our bookshelf and pulled down the tattered Polish-English dictionary that sat on the highest shelf. I sat cross legged on the floor, holding my breath as I flipped the pages from A to Z to find the mysterious word. I turned to the last page.

Zyd meant Jew.

3 Dirty Deeds Done Dirt Cheap

The unpleasant trip down memory lane to St. Wojciech's did nothing to get my mood out of the toilet. Some memories should be laid to rest forever. But thanks to Lenny's meddling, I couldn't stop thinking about St. Wojciech's and that damn Polish-English dictionary. By the time I arrived at the Zodiac Agency, I was exhausted and my nerves were frazzled from sitting in Beltway traffic for forty five minutes with Archie whining in my ear.

I heard Bosco, Zodiac's owner, cursing me before I walked through the office door.

"Ronson, you're a friggin' hour late!" he bellowed. The earthworm-like veins on his temples looked like they were about to burst. "And don't give me lip about getting stuck in traffic. If you weren't a weak little girl, I'd make you drop and give me twenty."

Bosco resembled Jabba the Hutt after a three day bender. His sweaty bald head sat atop a four-hundred-pound body that looked to be made out of fleshy Play-Doh. I it was hard to believe that Bosco had once been a decorated cop.

"What makes you think I can't do that?" I said, rolling up my sleeves. "How about we see who can do the most push ups in five minutes? You man enough Bosco, you big pussy?"

I got down on the dirty floor and cranked out twenty one-armed push ups. I I liked winding Bosco up until he threw a temper tantrum and threatened to fire me. The threat was all the leverage Bosco had, which made me eager to egg him on.

"Get up before I come over and show you how I do push ups with my dick," Bosco grumbled. I wiped my hands on my jeans, sat down on the hard plastic chair across from his cluttered desk and stared over Bosco's head at the bumper-to-bumper traffic on York Road.

"You're a real smart ass," Bosco said, scratching his arm pit. "That's why I'm giving you this special assignment." He shot me an evil smile and tossed a thick sheaf of papers at me.

I pushed the papers back across the desk. "I don't have time to digest this bullshit. Break the job down for me, Bosco."

"OK girlie, you're going to tail Mackenzie Peters-Royce. She's a freshman at Loyola College and the daughter of City Council member Maurice Royce. Her daddy believes his little girl is hooking up with her married English professor." Bosco slid me a blurry picture of a middle-aged man with his arm around a teenage girl.

"These are the love birds. Your assignment is to find out where they're doing the nasty, get some pictures, and then report back to me. I need a full report by the end of the week or else you're—"

"Lemme guess, fired?" I huffed. "Why don't you just fire me and put us both out of our misery? This job stinks worse than Archie's farts."

Sneaking around cheap motels to spy on pervy college professors and hot-to-trot spoiled teenagers was my idea of hell. This job was really scraping the bottom of the barrel, even for a bottom feeder like Bosco.

"What his job needs is a woman's touch, that's why I saved it for especially for you." Bosco licked his slimy lips and blew me a kiss. "Tell you what, if you can finish the job by Thursday I'll throw in an extra ten dollars."

"Ten fucking lousy dollars! You think you're doing me a favor by giving me a crap assignment?"

"Who's my number one girl?" Bosco taunted. "See you at the end of the week, superstar."

I kicked the door shut and stomped out. The sad part was that Bosco honestly thought he was doing me a favor by giving me this crap assignment. I had to quit

Zodiac before I lost my last bit of self-esteem.

I picked up a rock and threw it against the building. I kicked the tires of Bosco's car and fumed as I unlocked my Toyota. Archie jumped into the passenger seat and slobbered stinky dog kisses over my face. He always knew I was being kicked around. I felt so low that I didn't even try to push Archie away when he forced his eighty-five-pound body into my lap.

"This is the last shitty job I'm doing for Zodiac, Archie. Let's get the hell out of here and head to the dog park."

When Bosco had his aneurysm, I sure as hell wasn't going to call 911.

4 A Deadly Sin

I smoked cigarette after cigarette and listened to Black Sabbath's greatest hits through my headphones at top volume. While Ozzy Osbourne wailed, I stamped my feet to prevent them from turning into icy stumps while I ruminated about how much I hated this low-life private detective crap. Archie snoozed in the back seat, oblivious to my dark mood.

Bosco's assignment was worse than I imagined. Sitting in my car in the lot of a run down motel on Pulaski Highway was hell on Earth. I proceeded to spend a bone-chilled night waiting for Mackenzie Peters-Royce to emerge from one of the rent-by-the hour rooms so I could videotape her with her Humbert Humbert boyfriend.

Just before sunrise I gave up. Had Bosco had given me the wrong information?—a strong possibility because his informants were usually junkies. Had the couple fled the flea bag motel while I was taking a pee? Either way, my take-home pay for twelve hours equaled zero. I texted two words to Bosco: "I quit."

At six am, I pulled into a convenience store. With only three measly dollars in my pocket, I had to dig under the car seats to scrounge up enough change for breakfast.

I slurped down half my sludgy coffee then tossed the rest out the window. I took one bite out of a jelly donut, it was dry as a cracker. I offered it to Archie who gobbled it down in one bite. I wished I had enough money for a real meal to fill our growling stomachs, but with only fifteen cents left I couldn't even afford a pack of gum.

At the condo, I found Don doing bicep curls in his Baltimore City Police Department Pistol Team T-shirt. His private parts bulged in time with his meaty biceps as he counted out his repetitions.

"Hey good looking," he beamed at me. "Check this out."

Don stripped off his T-shirt to show off his buff chest. He flexed his pectoral muscles making his nipples jiggle like water drops sizzling on a skillet.

"You like?" he said, doing his best Arnold Schwarzenegger imitation.

Don's buck naked body made my nipples perk up like they'd been doused with ice cubes. I loved the way he made me feel like a horny teenager, especially when he acted like a cheesy Chippendale's dancer.

Over the past four months, we hadn't had time for sex, let alone the crazy, off the hook sex we were good at. Don had been logging as much overtime as his sergeant would allow. "Gotta begin putting away money for our future, babe," he'd say apologetically after pulling another double shift. Every night he hit the sack and left me sad, hot, and bothered.

Dog Spelled Backwards

I glanced at the kitchen clock. Don had . forty minutes before he had to report for roll call—enough time for a quick wham, bam, thank you ma'am. I hadn't showered and was hungry enough to eat Archie's kibble, but I didn't want to miss this tiny window to get down and dirty.

Don read my mind. "You're overdressed for the occasion," he said, pulling off my T-shirt and jeans. "I'm charging you with indecent exposure and putting on the handcuffs."

In one motion, Don swooped me into the bedroom and tumbled me onto the king sized bed. We laughed like a pair of over-sexed sixteen-year-olds left alone for the first time. Don pulled me close and stroked my thigh. "We need to meet like this more often."

"Clock's ticking, officer," I teased, licking Don's ear and kicking off my underwear. Archie hopped onto the bed and wedged his misshaped head in between us. I pushed him off with my foot. "Jealousy is a deadly sin," I scolded. Archie let out a low growl then curled up in a tight ball on his own bed.

Don and I were just about to get to triple X-rated when the doorbell rang. Archie barked and growled like the house was on fire. He ran in tight circles at the foot of the bed, slobbering and whining. I moaned as the door bell continued ringing.

"Guess playtime is over," Don said giving me a playful slap on my butt. "I need to grab a cold shower to take me down a few notches. Can't show up for roll call with this at full attention," he laughed, pointing at his crotch.

I threw on my clothes and reached for a cigarette. Who else but Lenny could have the bad timing to ruin my sex life.

"Dammit Lenny!" I shouted down the stairs. "I'm going to beat the living daylights out of you."

Archie and I marched down the stairs in lockstep. "You have permission to bite!" I said. "But wait for my command."

I balled my fists, ready to deck Lenny. I counted to three then opened the door. There stood Lenny, a shit-eating grin on his face and a shopping bag in his outstretched arms.

"Shabbat shalom!" he said "I brought apple cake."

I slammed the door in his face.

"It's cold out here." Lenny bellowed, his voice muffled but insistent. "I walked all the way from Reisterstown Road. Please let me in!"

"Bad timing. You ever think of calling first?" I yelled through the front door.

"I can't use the phone on the Sabbath, Jane," Lenny relied. "It's a sin."

"It's a sin that you are such a pain in my ass. What do you want?"

"Rabbi Goldberg wants to hire you."

"Who the hell is Rabbi Goldberg? Why does he want to hire me?"

"Rabbi Goldberg is my Torah teacher. I told him you're the best private investigator in Baltimore. Here's his business card."

Lenny piled it on thick. I was broke and jobless, so why not talk business with a rabbi?

I cracked the door open just enough so Lenny couldn't get inside. "Gimme that card," I hissed. Lenny slipped it through the crack.

"Can I please come in?" he whined. "I have to use the bathroom, it's an emergency."

I rolled my eyes and opened the door. "You have one minute to pee then get out. Understand?

"Of course. Could I get a drink of water first?"

"Do your business then scram, you pathetic weasel."

Lenny knew I was bluffing. There was no way he was leaving anytime soon now that I'd let him inside. I grabbed the shopping bag as Lenny hurried to the bathroom.

The scent of the apple cake made my mouth water and my stomach start growling all over again. At least I would have something to eat for breakfast. I sat down at my kitchen table and cut a thick piece of cake. Then I examined the rabbi's card. One side was written in Hebrew. I

Dog Spelled Backwards

flipped the card over to the English side. It read:

Rabbi Avram Goldberg

Torah Scholar/Businessman

What kind of rabbi hires a private detective, I wondered, wolfing down the apple cake.

5 Stranger in a Strange Land

I fed Archie a can of his favorite wet dog food, the slimy kind that smelled like a landfill in August. The more food stunk, the better Archie liked it. He licked his grimy chops and belched. I flopped on the couch. Archie jumped on my lap and I scratched him behind his erect ears. Within seconds, his triangle-shaped eyes closed and he was snoring like a brace of lumberjacks.

I was just about to doze off when Lenny tapped me on the shoulder. Archie and I both jerked awake.

"I thought I told you to empty your bladder then hit the road."

"Tomorrow I've set up an appointment with Rabbi Goldberg. He is eager to meet you."

I'd never met a rabbi, much less an Orthodox one. There'd be rules of etiquette I was bound to mess up and all sorts of other things I didn't know squat about.

Ever since Lenny dropped the bomb-shell that we were Jewish, a small part of me wanted to find out more about my back-ground. But I wasn't ready to talk to any rabbis about it.

"Riddle me this genius," I said. "If being Jewish is such a big deal, why did my mother hide being Jewish for so long? And why is religion so important to you?"

Lenny teared up. "You don't understand. All of my life, I've felt like there was something missing, like I didn't know who I was or what I was supposed to believe. Now that I know I'm Jewish, I finally know where I am going in life and how to get there."

"Please stop Lenny. You sound like an outtake from an Oprah episode. I think I hear

Barry Manilow music playing in the background. Besides, I'm steering clear of religion, but for money I'll work with anyone–Jews, Muslims, Christians or even devil worshippers. Does the rabbi pay cash?"

"Why are you so hard, Jane? It wouldn't kill you to get a little religion. It might soften you up a bit so you wouldn't be so cranky all the time. And maybe being part of a religious community would help you make some friends. If it wasn't for Don, Archie and me, you'd be completely cut off from society. That's not a healthy way to go through life. Besides, Don is excited that you are going to have a Jewish wedding.... hey, stop pushing!"

I shoved him out the door. I'd take the rabbi's assignment, but I wasn't going to listen to Lenny lecture me one second longer.

The next day, I drove my ancient Toyota down Churchill Parkway and turned right onto lower Park Heights Avenue where I passed greasy carry-out restaurants selling lake trout and storefronts that advertised sleazy check cashing operations. Minutes later, I entered Westwood, home to Baltimore's Jewish Orthodox community. Men in black suits and black fedoras strolled down the sidewalks. Some of them wore white prayer shawls that flapped in the strong breeze. Alongside the men, women in dark clothes and fancy hats pushed double and triple baby strollers. Little boys in starched white shirts and girls in pinafores skipped behind their parents.

As I drove deeper into Westwood I passed synagogue after synagogue. In between were religious schools and businesses selling kosher food, religious books and stores with cryptic Hebrew lettering. I passed a restaurant with a blinking "Glatt Kosher Chinese Food and Sushi" neon sign.

Rabbi Goldberg had texted me directions, but I still couldn't find his house. After passing the enormous Jewish Community Center, I turned down a narrow side street. The ramshackle brick houses looked the same and none of them posted street numbers. Rusty tricycles, abandoned dolls and broken chairs were scattered on the weedy lawns. Dented cargo vans sat in the driveways and scores of mini vans were haphazardly parked along the street.

After fifteen minutes of searching for the rabbi's house, I parked the car and walked towards Park Heights Avenue. I spotted a woman across the road. Her head was wrapped in a scarf. She wore a long coat, and held a baby in her arms. I trotted across the street. The woman avoided my eyes and clutched the infant close to her breast.

"Excuse me," I said, standing in front of her. "I'm looking for Rabbi Goldberg."

Her horrified face took me aback. Did she think I'd snatch her child and sink fangs into its flesh?

Still avoiding eye contact, the woman skirted around me and backed away.

"Where is Rabbi Goldberg's house?" I demanded. "Do you understand English?"

The woman high tailed it down the street and without looking back, pointed to a nondescript house.

Dog Spelled Backwards

"Thanks for all your help!" I screamed after her in my most pissed off voice.

I climbed the crumbling marble stoop and rang the dirty doorbell. A small, hand-written sign in the smeared window next to the door read "Bait Yerushalayim."

While I waited, my sixth sense kicked in. I was being spied on. I wheeled around to see a group of children on the sidewalk. I met the stern gaze of the oldest child—a boy about eight. Hanging from his baseball cap, he had what looked like baby dread-locks. Four little girls dressed in matching dresses and white knee socks stood nearby. They all had red hair and freckles; probably related. None of them smiled. When another girl peeked out from behind the boy, I stuck out my tongue. They ran and hid behind a tree, except for the oldest boy who stood erect and put up his dukes like a pint-sized prizefighter. Just then, Rabbi Goldberg opened the door.

"Miss Ronson, I presume."

I went to shake his hand. He shoved it in his pocket. Didn't he have manners? Then I remembered Lenny telling me that Orthodox men only touch their wives.

"Welcome to my house and the Bait Yerushalayim *shtiebel*," said Rabbi Goldberg, waving me inside.

I paused before stepping into a hallway that smelled of floor wax and chicken soup. A chorus of angry voices emanated from deep in the house. The boy followed me inside. He kept staring at me like I had three heads. I wasn't sure how to handle the little brat in the presence of a rabbi.

"Enough with the staring," the rabbi shouted over his shoulder. "Get your sisters, it's time for lunch."

He turned to me. "Excuse my children. I've told them not to stare at non-Jews."

"Don't they see non-Jews at their school?"

"Oh no!" said the Rabbi. "My children go to *yeshivas*, Jewish religious schools to learn the Torah and other traditional texts. Sometimes they study a little literature, but who needs Shakespeare when we have a biblical rock star like Abraham?"

Dog Spelled Backwards

Abraham a rock star? I thought about making a Jesus Christ Superstar joke but held my tongue.

"In my office, we can chat in private," said the Rabbi.

The floor creaked ominously as I followed the Rabbi down the narrow hallway. On my left, in what might have been a dining room, a dozen men in black jackets and white, open collar shirts hunched over a table, arguing at the top of their lungs. The men all sported unkempt woodsmen's beards. One man jumped up, caterwauling in what I assumed was Hebrew. He held an open prayer-book in one hand and jabbed his finger across the page. With every shout, a staccato of spittle sprayed in the air, and his strange dreadlocks shook like a tangle of hairy wind chimes. Another frowned and raised his finger to the ceiling, shouting and stamping his feet.

Suddenly, all the men were on their feet, shouting and gesturing. A tea cup skittered across the table and smashed into bits against the wooden floor. There was no mistaking their passion for religion as they argued. The scene was almost as good as a bar fight.

Just then, the man with the longest dreadlocks stopped shouting. He pounded his fist on the table and turned to me.

"Who let this *shiksa* in?" he said, wrinkling his nose like he'd smelled a fart. "And why is she staring at us?"

"Bad day at the synagogue?" I snorted.

"Calm down Yehuda," the Rabbi said. The man grunted disapprovingly and sat down.

The Rabbi turned to me. "Miss Ronson, you are witnessing a debate about the finer points of Jewish law. These gentlemen are engaged the highest form of Jewish learning. Rabbi Bublanski questions whether it is forbidden to carry a baby in one's arms on the Sabbath since this act could be construed as labor, which is strictly forbidden on this holy day. The other gentleman says he is misinterpreting the prohibition against carrying on the Sabbath; that it is not a sin to hold an infant. Rabbi Bublanski points out that carrying a baby on the Sabbath could lead to Jews carrying other objects, such as umbrellas, or God forbid money, a sin of the highest order."

My mouth hung open. All this hooting and hollering about carrying a baby?

The Rabbi wagged his finger in my face. "If you don't close your mouth you'll catch flies," he scolded.

6 A Bad Apple

I took a step into Rabbi Goldberg's tiny office and froze. From the battered wooden floor to the rotting dropped ceiling, all I could see were books piled upon books. I was afraid they'd collapse and suffocate me if I made one false move. There was no place to sit down much less stand.

With a wiggle of his well-padded hips, Rabbi Goldberg shimmied past me and stood behind a beaten up wooden desk stacked with papers. He bent over and pushed aside a ziggurat of books to reveal a sliver of desktop, then sat down with his hands folded over his ample gut. "Like Moses parting the Red Sea" he laughed.

"Pinchas, I need a chair for our guest!" he bellowed in the direction of the hallway.

"Forget it, Rabbi. I'll stand," I said.

"As you wish. Now let's get down to business."

Something scraped the wooden floor behind me. A sullen teenage boy dragged a beat up chair toward me. He had a blonde crew cut and wore a clean white T-shirt with white fringes sticking out from under it. Colorful tattoos of fire-breathing dragons and curlicued tribal designs covered his bare arms. I spied a neck tattoo of a spider peeking out from under his collar. The kid looked more out of place at the Rabbi's house than I did.

"We don't need the chair after all. Get back to your studying," the Rabbi scolded. The kid eyed my Ramones T-shirt and smiled. "I used to love that band" he said softly with a faraway look in his eyes before shuffling off.

"Is he Orthodox?"

"Not all Orthodox have *payis*, or dreadlocks as *goyim*—non Jews—call them, the Rabbi explained. "Pinchas used to be called Travis. He was a good kid, went to synagogue and Hebrew school. Then he turned bad. He ran with a gang and was arrested for selling drugs. He almost overdosed a few times. After he got out of rehab his mother brought him to me to straighten him out. Now he's learning with us and wants to be a rabbi. We call Travis a *bal tshuva*, someone who has returned to Judaism."

With all the strange Hebrew terms being thrown at me, it was a good thing I had a photographic memory, otherwise I'd be completely lost. I made a mental note to download a Hebrew-English dictionary app to my iPhone.

I gave Rabbi Goldberg the once over. I pegged him to be about forty. His penetrating blue eyes were magnified by his hipster, wire-rim glasses. I eyed his scraggly black beard that ended at his Adam's apple like an untrimmed hedge. His *payis* were tucked behind small, elfin ears.

Dog Spelled Backwards

"What's the deal with the black market kidneys? What do you need me to do?"

"We have bad apples in our community Miss Ronson," the Rabbi said, steepling his fingers against his thin lips and leaning back in his chair. "I need you to get information about certain people without the police getting involved. You give me the reports, videos, print outs of emails—don't leave out any details. Once you've compiled a thorough dossier, I'll take it from there. We Jews like to take care of our own problems on our own terms."

"You've got my full attention Rabbi. I can be discrete."

"I should hope so, and shouldn't you be taking notes?" Rabbi Goldberg asked, looking at my biker chick attire. He shot a disapproving look at my studded belt and black leather wristband. It didn't phase me. I was used to people thinking of me as a freak. Anyway, the Rabbi looked like a weirdo to me.

"I have an eidetic memory," I said, tapping my temple. "I don't need to write anything down. It's all stored in my mental hard drive. Keep talking."

He nodded and continued. "Do you have any idea how long the wait is for a healthy kidney? My uncle Moishe of blessed memory was on the waiting list for a kidney for two years. He died at Sinai Hospital waiting for a donor. It's not so easy to find a perfect match. Family members aren't always the right fit. And hoping for someone to die so you can get their healthy kidneys—it's like winning the lottery, a total long shot. If you're not there when the phone rings they go right to the next person. Uncle Moishe didn't leave his house for fear of missing the call that a donor had been found. If I could have given him my kidney, believe me, I would have done it in a heartbeat."

He choked back a tear. "It's no wonder people want kidneys, no matter where they come from. Who wants to be on dialysis for years? We Jews believe that to save a life is the highest commandment. Am I getting through to you?"

"Yeah, it must suck to wait for a kidney." I said, unmoved. "What does this have to do with me?"

"There's a certain rabbi in our community who is preying on Jewish men and women who need kidney transplants. These people are desperate. They'll pay top dollar for a matching kidney—no questions asked. But that's just the first step. Once you've got the kidney, you need a doctor to perform the operation. And then you need the right drugs so that your body doesn't reject the kidney," he added, reaching into his desk draw and extracting a can of Red Bull and taking a long swallow.

The rabbi fixed me a hard stare. "This rabbi is a real *mamzer*, a bastard who'd cut his own mother's heart out for a nickel. Unfortunately, this *mamzer* is also my cousin; a family member, imagine! He charges fifty- thousand dollars in cash for a kidney and ten thousand dollars for the operation, plus more money for medications. He's been doing this for years and is wealthy beyond belief. He owns houses in Florida, Israel and Los Angeles.

Worse, he drives a German car—an Audi! I smell the concentration camp ovens every time I even think of a German car."

He took another slug of the energy drink. "People say has a wife and family in Rio de Janeiro *and* a wife and seven children here in Baltimore."

I cracked my knuckles. "Where does he get the kidneys?"

"Dundalk, China—who knows? Once he gets his the kidneys he has a list of crooked doctors who perform back alley operations. In fact, there is a makeshift operating room right here in this very neighborhood."

The rabbi stood up and leaned toward me, his face inches from mine. I noted a faint scar running from the corner of this mouth to his left ear.

"I want this man stopped Miss Ronson— and you are going to help me do it."

"Who's this *mamzer*?" I asked.

"His name is Solomon Dworkin but everyone calls him Solly. He holds court at Horowitz Bagels on Reisterstown Road making deals and meeting with his kidney clients. I want you get as much hard evidence about his kidney selling activities as possible. I'll gladly pay top dollar for every scrap of information; every photo, email, license plate number and cocktail napkin you can lay your hands on."

"How will I recognize him?" I pictured myself walking into the bagel joint and into a sea of identical men in black suits with beards.

"Dworkin never operates alone," the Rabbi replied, self-consciously running his hand over his scar. "He's always got an armed Russian bodyguard named Yuri, an ex-bodybuilder and full-time thug at his side. Oy vey, this man is evil. When he's not trafficking in kidneys he's selling steroids to high school students. I've heard rumors that he runs a prostitution ring out of the Kiev Nights Supper Club on Seven Mile Lane."

"Are you up to this?" Goldberg said. "I need an answer right away. Your cousin Asher Lev says you are a very resourceful private investigator and you are fearless. Those are exactly the qualities I need."

The more Goldberg talked, the more excited I got. I liked the idea of taking on a knucklehead Russian and doing some real detective work rather than the bullshit Bosco had been feeding me. This was my type of assignment.

But who was the rabbi talking about? I only had one cousin, and his name was Lenny, not Asher Lev. Was Lenny going by a code name?

Rabbi Goldberg sensed my confusion. "We refer to Lenny by his true Hebrew name, Asher Lev," he replied. The Rabbi finished the rest of the Red Bull, crushed the can against his desk and flung it into an overflowing wastebasket.

"By the way, do you have a permit for that gun?"

I always carried a Ruger GP .357 in a vest holster. He must have seen the outline under my T-shirt.

"Have licensed gun, will hunt bad guys," I said, patting my holster.

Dog Spelled Backwards

"I accept your assignment. By the way Rabbi, do I detect a five shot, .22 mini revolver in *you*r shoulder holster? My spidey sense tells me that scar is from a knife fight. How am I doing so far?"

He nodded. "Very good Miss Ronson. You know seem to know a thing or two about guns. That will be extremely helpful in taking on Dworkin and the Russian. And yes, the knife wound is from many years ago. Sometimes Torah arguments get a little heated."

That was bullshit. The scar was definitely from some kind of street fight. I decided to let sleeping dogs lie—for now.

"One more thing before I commit, Rabbi. I charge a hundred dollars an hour and you cover all of my expenses, no questions asked."

"Not a problem, Miss Ronson," the rabbi said smiling. He tossed the bankroll to me.

"Here's three thousand to get you started."

I caught the money and shoved it in my back pocket.

The rabbi stood up. "Let's consider our arrangement off the books. Expect a call from my wife tomorrow morning. You'll need help with your appearance for this assignment."

"What does my appearance have to do with getting the job done?" I couldn't picture myself in anything but my normal uniform of black jeans, rock and roll T-shirts and my motorcycle jacket.

"Let's just say that you're going to need to go shopping so you look like a nice Jewish girl, and not a teenage boy."

"Whatever Rabbi, it's your dime."

"Pinchas will see you out. It's a pleasure doing business with such an *interesting* Jewish woman."

"I'm not Jewish!" I blurted out, annoyed that the Rabbi was baiting me. Why was everyone challenging my identity? And even if Lenny was right, that I was Jewish, what did it matter? Didn't anyone mind their own damn business anymore?

"We'll discuss your Judaism later," the Rabbi said waving me off. "Get me the information on Dworkin ASAP."

I walked back down the hallway, the scuffed wooden floor creaked under my boots. The room where the men had been studying was now empty. Pinchas stood by the front door.

"Rabbi Goldberg is some piece of work," I said, trying to make conversation.

"You don't know the half of it," Pinchas mumbled, gazing at this sneakers. He held the door open for me to leave.

"Go with God," he said, lifting his eyes briefly to meet mine. "And watch your back."

7 Marry Me, Jane

A million questions buzzed around in my head as I drove back to the condo. What kind of Rabbi has a gangster scar on his face, carries a gun, and lies? And why would he hire me to rat out another rabbi?

I was being played, but couldn't figure out the how's or why's just yet. Worse, my stupid cousin Lenny was involved. Leave it to Lenny to stir up a shit storm and then come crying to me when he needed to be rescued.

I nudged my battered Toyota through the stop-and-go traffic along Falls Road. Don would be home any minute for dinner. I was determined to give him a hot meal, even if it came courtesy of the Mt. Jefferson Pizza and Sub Shoppe.

I picked up an extra large pizza with a side order of cheese fries and a liter of Coke. I'd just bitten into a second slice of gooey pizza and was slipping Archie my crust when Don walked in with a grocery bag.

"Looks like you've been slaving over a hot oven all day," he said, eyeing the pizza hungrily.

"Archie and I will eat this whole pie, unless you dig in fast."

"I bought you something special." Don pulled a gallon of chocolate chip ice cream out of a grocery bag. "Sweets for my sweetheart."

Don frowned, sensing my bad mood. "Bosco been yanking your chain again?"

"I told him to stuff it. My pain in the ass cousin's got me working for a Rabbi. Can you believe that?"

"As long as you're not breaking any laws, I don't care who you're working for."

Don and I were night and day. He was a straight arrow cop who followed procedures to the letter. Like Superman, Don tood for truth, justice and the American Way. I challenged authority and never met a rule I didn't want to break. I lived in a world where bad guys and good guys were hard to tell apart.

Professionally, we kept to a strict "need to know" policy about our jobs. The less we knew about each other's business, the better.

"Eat some of this pizza," I said. "Or I'll eat it for you."

"I know you will," Don laughed. "And you'll grow an extra set of love handles."

"You know it's metabolically impossible for me to gain weight," I taunted.

Don waved me off. "I'm not hungry for pizza right now. I'm going for this ice cream, dessert's the best part."

He grabbed two spoons and sat on the couch. He waited for me to join him while I crammed down another slice. I wiped my mouth and flopped onto the couch next to him. I snuggled against Don's buff chest and reached for the ice cream. After I'd taken a few spoonfuls of melting chocolate from the carton on his lap, Don squirmed and dug into his pocket.

"Digging for gold?" I joked. "We can play hide the salami after we finish our ice cream."

"For once in your life, please be serious," Don said, tenderly putting his sticky hand in mine and pressing it against his heart.

"Stop eating. I have a very important question."

I glanced at the small black box resting on the couch between us. My mouth dried out and my heart pounded. More than once I'd been told that I had the emotional IQ of a desk lamp. But even though I wasn't a girly girly who watched stupid romantic comedies, I sure as hell knew what was in that box.

Don cradled the box in his hand and gazed into my eyes. "I've loved you ever since I laid eyes on you," he intoned.

I watched in shock as Don removed a sparkly, heart-shaped diamond ring out of the box then got down on one knee.

"I'm a cop, I don't talk much about my feelings, so I'll cut to the chase. I'm asking if you can find it in your messy, dark, complicated heart..." He swallowed hard, "to be my wife. And more than that, the mother of our children. Will you do me the extreme honor of wearing this engagement ring and marrying me?"

My ears roared and my body twitched as Don's lips moved. I felt like I was being sucked into outer space, shocked and paralyzed by indecision. All I could feel was the quart of chocolate ice cream melting on my lap and Archie's warm tongue lapping the drips. I didn't know whether to run away from Don or throw my arms around him.

Don snapped his fingers in front of my face. "Earth to Jane? Do you hear me?" He knitted his eyebrows and searched my blank face. "Jane? Do I need to call the paramedics?"

Dog Spelled Backwards

"Yes," I whispered.

"Yes, what? Do I need to take you to the hospital or yes, you will marry me?

"Yes, I'll put on the ring and marry you if that's what you want."

"What *I* want!" Don huffed. "Can you at least pretend you want to marry me?"

Deep down, I wanted to tell Don that I was happy, overjoyed that he had broken through my emotional firewalls and touched my icicle of a heart. Why couldn't I admit that I loved him? Was I irrevocably emotionally retarded?

I straightened up and collected myself. "What part of 'yes' don't you understand? Gimme that ring."

I wiggled the ring on my index finger and shoved it under Don's nose.

"Babe, the ring goes on *this* finger," Don said, carefully sliding the ring over the knuckle of my fourth finger and holding it in place for me to admire. It fit perfectly. I turned the ring round and round, then held it to the light. The facets glittered like hundreds of tiny mirrors. The ring must have cost a fortune. I couldn't stop smiling.

A small voice in my head said, "Welcome to the adult world. You are now a member of the normal club. Don't screw up."

"Do you like the ring?" Don asked. "Lenny helped me pick it out. He said you'd like this one best. But you can exchange it."

So Don and Lenny had been in cahoots. I wondered how long they'd planned to get this ring on my finger. Did they go to a jewelry store and giggle like high school girls on a shopping spree?

"I love it," I said, my hand quivering. "And yeah, I love you. Now let's stop talking about our feelings and polish off that ice cream."

Don kissed me passionately. "I've got another quart of Rocky Road in the freezer with your name on it Mrs. Williams."

I blushed. "Just promise me you aren't arranging a big church wedding," I pleaded. "You know how I feel about religion. Can we run away to Vegas and get married by an Elvis impersonator?"

Don turned serious. "No Janey. We need to honor your mother's wishes according to her will. Didn't you read that part? It has to be a Jewish wedding."

8 Wigged Out

The day after Don proposed to me, I stood naked in the kitchen drinking coffee and staring at my engagement ring. Don sat at the kitchen table in his underwear reading the Baltimore Sun.

The shock of wearing a diamond ring on my left finger and having said yes to his proposal hadn't yet worn off. I felt like I was living in a parallel universe where normal people did things like get married, own condos and think about having kids.

I'd stayed up all night in a daze eating potato chips and wondering why I said yes to Don. I finally crawled into bed at four am and watched Don and Archie sleep. As usual Archie was curled in a ball in the crook of Don's knees.

I was deep in my coffee reverie when a car horn blasted. "You know anyone who drives a blue Dodge Caravan?" Don called out. The driver continued leaning on the horn.

Don scowled. "If they don't shut up I'm gonna flash them my badge."

"Damn it. I'll get rid of them," I said, throwing on a bathrobe.

I opened the front door. Before me where two unsmiling women in ankle-length skirts and long-sleeved black sweaters. Their arms were folded over their chests and their heads were covered with unstylish hats that looked liked they came from the bottom of the Salvation Army bargain bins.

"Are you Jane Ronson?" the taller one said. She staring disapprovingly at my left breast poking out of my bathrobe.

I met her gaze. "I'm Jane. Who the hell are you?" Archie was at my side emitting low growls, ready to attack if I said the word.

"I'm Shayna, Rabbi Goldberg's wife and this is my sister Miriam," she said, peering over my shoulder.

I turned, Don stood buck naked with his hands on his hips wearing his sternest cop face. "You OK?" he asked.

"Stand down Don. I got this," I answered as Archie continued growling.

"What do you want?" I said angrily. "I'm in the middle of something." Miriam pantomimed for me to me to close my robe. I ignored her.

"My husband has already explained that you need to go undercover to expose the black market kidney ring that is bringing shame to our community. We're here to take you shopping so you can look like a proper Orthodox Jewish woman. After one look at you, I see I've got my work cut out for me." She wrung her hands, scrunched up her chubby face and raised her eyes skyward. "Oy vey, why is God punishing me?"

"Wait a minute drama queen," I hissed. "You come barging into *my* house unannounced and now you're lecturing me about *my* lifestyle! Get the hell out of here and don't let the door slam you in the ass."

"I think you might want to reconsider," Shayna said cooly.

"Why shouldn't I throw you both out?"

She patted her handbag. "I've got a thousand dollars cash for you."

I chewed the inside of my cheek. Shayna knew she had me. I badly needed that money. For as long as I could remember, I'd been living hand-to-mouth. After my father died, my mother was left penniless. She cleaned the houses of Mt. Jefferson's rich families, mended their clothes and did whatever other odd jobs she could cobble together to keep the two of us afloat.

I hated being poor, and the kids at the Mt. Jefferson Elementary school never let me forget that even though we shared the same zip code, I wasn't from their social class.

"All right," I said, exhaling furiously. "Hand over the money."

"I knew you'd see it my way," Shanya retorted, slipping me the bankroll. "Now get dressed and be in our van in three minutes or I'll drag you in there myself."

I was taken aback. Nobody spoke to me like that. I fingered the money. I knew there was more to be had if I could just play around with this bullshit charade.

"Gimme five minutes sister," I said chugging down the last of my coffee.

I rode in the back seat of the van shoehorned between Miriam and a tall, skinny woman who introduced herself as Malka, Shayna's sister-in-law. "We're so happy to help you become religious," Malka said smiling at me.

I smiled back wanly as I gave Malka the once over. The woman wore black, military-issued glasses perched at the tip of her carrot-like nose. Her knobby knees poked out from beneath her voluminous skirt.

By contrast, Miriam was as corpulent as a sumo wrestler. Her love handles overflowed the sides of her skirt and her enormous breasts swayed like water balloons as Shayna zoomed around the slow moving cars on Reisterstown Road.

Even though Westwood bordered Mt. Jefferson, I rarely set foot there. Westwood was hard core Orthodox territory with pockets of newly-arrived Russians and sprinkling of Latinos. William Donald Schaefer Road, Westwood's main drag, was lined with Kosher bakeries, Kosher butchers, Kosher restaurants, tailors, watchmakers and small storefronts selling Jewish religious items. It wasn't the kind of neighborhood that had anything to offer a person like me.

Shayna accelerated into a narrow alley behind a row of forlorn stores. She pulled up in front of a loading dock and slammed the brakes. "Get out," she ordered.

We walked toward a door marked "Kaplan's Sheitel Emporium."

"Why aren't we going in the front door?" Malka asked tentatively.

"I don't want anyone seeing us bringing *this*," she gestured haughtily in my direction," type of person into Kaplan's," Shayna sniffed. "They have a reputation to maintain."

Malka put her arm around my waist to guide me in. "Hands off Olive Oyl," I hissed. We walked in the store and were immediately greeted by a tiny woman with an ill-fitting beehive wig atop her tiny head.

"Hello Mrs. Kaplan," Shayna bellowed.

"Shayna, darling, you don't have to shout, I'm not deaf. How nice to see you again. You need a new *sheitel* for your daughter's wedding?"

It took a second before I registered on her radar screen.

"Who is this wild animal you've brought into my store?" Mrs. Kaplan said wide-eyed. "Is this a boy *goy* or a girl *goy*?"

"This is a girl," Shayna sighed, rolling her eyes. " And she's Jewish."

"Oh dear," Mrs. Kaplan murmured. "I guess we've got our work cut out for us."

"First thing, we need to get her a *sheitel*," Shayna demanded.

"What's a *sheitel?* I asked, ready to deck Shayna if she tried anything funny.

"It's a wig," Shayna replied, adjusting what I realized was a wig on her head then pointing to the rows of be-wigged mannequins that filled the small store. "It's not *tznuis* for married Orthodox women to show their hair. Only your husband should see your real hair in the privacy of your own home." Shayna re-adjusted her Marcia Brady-like wig. "We can't have you dressing like you have no sense of decency."

"*Tznuis*. I mocked. "It sounds like you're sneezing."

"Go ahead and laugh," Shayna said, crossing her arms and glaring at me. "*Tznuis* is a cornerstone of Orthodox Judaism," she lectured. "Rachel, the wife of the great Rabbi Akiva, gave up all of her riches and even sold her beautiful hair in the name of modesty and to pay for her husband to study Torah. It's said that Rachel was so modest she stuck pins in her calves so her skirt wouldn't lift above her kneecaps. For her modesty and great respect for Torah, Rabbi Akiva rewarded Rachel with a gold crown. Jewish woman make such sacrifices in the name of God because God rewards the righteous."

I flinched at the thought of pins being stuck through my calves. No matter how much money Rabbi Goldberg was paying me, it wasn't enough to put up with this crap. I was already sick being ridiculed for not being *tznuis*, as Shayna explained, the Orthodox Jewish principle of modesty that ruled everything from how short a woman's sleeves could be, to forbidding men to hear a woman sing for fear it would be sexually arousing.

Shayna plopped a frosted pageboy wig on my head. The thing itched as if someone had stretched an unwashed horse blanket over my scalp then injected fire ants into my hair follicles. All I wanted to do was pull it off my and head to the nearest bar. But I couldn't do that because Shayna and her posse stood guard over me like cats watching a mouse.

"Stop fiddling with that *sheitel*," scolded Shayna. "They all itch. Get used to it."

"Malka," she barked, "hand me the blonde Boro Park Special with the bangs."

In one motion, Shayna pulled the wig off my head. Before I could exhale she mashed the Boro Park Special on my head and began fussing with the bangs.

"What do you think, Miriam?" Shayna said admiringly as Malka nodded her ostrich-like head. "She almost looks like she could pass for Orthodox. Now it's time to get her out of those boy's clothes."

Sometimes the easiest thing to do is surrender, I thought as I took off my jeans, tank top and Doc Marten boots. I stood before Shayna in just my bikini underpants. I covered my tiny breasts with my hands.

"Is that a birthmark?" Malka asked, peering at my back through her Coke-bottle lens glasses.

"Take a good look Shayna," I said turning my back to her and spreading my arms out wide so they could take in the tattoo of a bleeding heart with a knife stuck through it that covered my entire back.

Malka and Miriam gripped each other's hands and backed away from me.

"I don't bite," I laughed. "But I think she does," I said, nodding toward Shayna who was busy rummaging through clothing racks and tossing items on the counter.

"Wear these," Shayna ordered. I reluctantly put on a long-sleeved starched white blouse with buttons up to my collar and a navy blue dirndl skirt that reached almost to my ankles. Black ballet flats and tan opaque stockings completed my transformation from punk rocker to proper Jewish girl. I took a long look at myself in the mirror. I didn't like what I saw. Why did I need to wear a wig along with these ugly clothes? It's not like any guy was going to notice me, trapped in a dingy wig shop deep in the bowels of Westwood.

Dog Spelled Backwards

"You have to be extremely careful. It's a sin for a Jewish man to look at a woman with intent to gain pleasure, even if he doesn't plan to do anything more than look." Shayna warned me when I tried rolling up my sleeves. "And you don't want the *goyim* staring at you either."

But I felt like a *goy:* a stranger slumming it among the Orthodox. Even though my mother was Jewish, which technically made me a Jew, I still wasn't considered exactly Kosher in the eyes of Shayna and her friends. They regarded me as an alien half-breed in need of religious guidance. If I told Shayna that I was raised Catholic she'd probably have a stroke.

"So *nu*, you think maybe we should just try a hat for her? Her hair is already short so that would be *tznuis*," Malka said timidly

"Forget the hat." Shayna shot Malka a withering look. "We're sticking with the *sheitel.*

9 Never on *Shabbos*

After four hours of trying on itchy wigs and clothing better suited for Amish grandmothers, Shayna and her posse finally wore me down. I'd bitten my nails down to the quicks and was close to fainting from fatigue and stress. After settling the bill and packing up the ugly clothing and wig in bulging shopping bags, Shayna loaded us all in the van for the ride back to my condo. I sat slumped like a sack of rice in the backseat.

"We are all proud of you for doing God's work," Malka cooed, handing me an energy bar and stroking my matted hair. "Next Friday night you will come to my house for *shabbos* dinner. We'll fatten you up with some chopped liver made with *schmaltz*." Miriam smiled and squeezed my hand. "We can't have you looking like a stick with legs. I'll make you some of my chicken soup with matzoh balls."

I was inches away from telling Rabbi Goldberg to shove it. This assignment was getting too weird and my self-confidence was wavering. I wasn't sure I could pass myself off as an Orthodox Jewish woman, much less one in need of a kidney transplant. As much as I desperately needed the money, sacrificing my dignity to do it wasn't my style. Wasn't that the reason I'd told Bosco to get lost?

I was happy to be out of Westwood and back in my own world. After Shayna dropped me off at my condo, I put the key into the lock and heard Archie barking furiously from the other side of the door. "I'm home, bruiser" I greeted as I opened the door. Archie planted his paws on my chest and slobbered kisses on my face.

I kicked off my clothes and stretched out on the king-sized bed in my underwear, idly channel surfing through the late afternoon talk shows. I wanted a beer but was too lazy to get one.

"Hey Archie, make like Spuds MacKenzie and fetch me a cold one from the fridge." Archie trotted over, picked up my T-shirt and tore it to shreds.

"Damn you!" I hopped off the bed and chased Archie around the room, finally tackling him as he jumped on the bed with shreds of cloth in his jaws. "You've ruined my favorite New York Dolls T-shirt! Don't you give a damn about classic punk rock?"

Archie looked at me thoughtfully, then grabbed a pair of Don's dirty socks and ran off. So much for my peaceful afternoon, it was time to get to work.

I booted up my laptop and searched the Internet for black market kidneys. I clicked through websites filled with pictures of bloody body parts: cadavers hacked up for their organs, emaciated men and women from Third World countries lifting their tattered shirts to show scars from selling their kidneys. I paused to light a cigarette then resumed my investigation.

Dog Spelled Backwards

I read that kidneys commanded as much as a hundred thousand dollars. The sicker people were, the less they cared how their replacement kidney was procured.

One company in China offered potential donors two thousand dollars, an iPad, and a trip to Tokyo Disneyland. Middlemen marked-up the organs to fifty thousand dollars, sometimes more.

I read about a hospital in India that catered to Americans and Canadians. The hospital boasted they would find a "humanitarian donor" for the price of sixty-five thousand dollars for the first kidney, and thirty five thousand for anyone needing a second kidney.

After coming across a picture of a teenage girl with a jagged scar from her armpit to her hip, I clicked off the computer in disgust.

Maybe Rabbi Goldberg did have a point about black market kidneys being morally wrong; maybe selling black market kidneys was a sin. It made me determined to figure out how I to present myself to Rabbi Dworkin so I could penetrate his operation.

But to do that I needed a cover story. I mulled it over for a few minutes until an idea came to me. I'd tell Rabbi Dworkin that I'd been diagnosed with advanced kidney disease and would die in six months without a transplant.

To make Dworkin really take the bait, I'd fib that I moved to Baltimore from California after my husband died leaving me with a small fortune. With a little help from make-up and enough up-front cash, I figured Dworkin would believe my sob story and try to sell me a kidney right away.

I texted Rabbi Goldberg that I needed cash for a down payment to Dworkin. Goldberg texted back:

Meet me at Jimmy's Restaurant in Fells Point in an hour. Convince me you're Orthodox.

Reluctantly, I dressed in the dowdy, long-sleeved blouse, gray, ankle-length skirt and cheap acrylic wig Shayna purchased for me. I studied myself in the full-length mirror and

Dog Spelled Backwards

gasped. I looked like a pilgrim having a bad hair day. Archie sniffed at my skirt and whined.

"Yeah, buddy. The things I do to keep you in kibble."

Fells Point was packed with tourists drinking themselves stupid in the rowdy bars along Thames Street. I headed to Jimmy's swathed in yards of dark fabric, the wretched wig on my head. I tripped on the cobblestones when my heel caught the hem of my skirt. "Shit!" I said. Then I bit my lip. I'd have to behave like a proper Jewish girl in front of Rabbi Goldberg.

I spotted Rabbi Goldberg the second I walked inside the restaurant. He sat with another Orthodox man at a far table next to a group of Johns Hopkins nurses just off the night shift chowing down on cheese steak subs and fried oysters washed down with pitchers of beer. The two men were deep in conversation when I approached. The other man looked up from his plate in horror and dropped his fork.

"She's joining us?" he gasped.

The man threw his napkin over his food and looked guiltily at his lap.

"Chill out Shlomo. She doesn't care that the crab cake you're eating isn't kosher. Just finish that *trafe* food before we go back to Westwood."

"Well," I said, turning full circle so the Rabbi could see my transformation. "Do I pass for Orthodox?"

He smiled. "Almost. The nose ring has to go." I cursed under my breath. I knew I'd forgotten something important. Good thing they couldn't see my tattoo.

"I'm meeting Dworkin tomorrow. I'll need money."

"Not so fast. Money can't change hands until Saturday night after *shabbos* ends. Tell Dworkin you'll meet him at Mazel Tov Kosher Pizza on Park Heights. Say your name is Ruth Moscowitz."

Rabbi Goldberg reached into his pocket and pulled out a thick wad of hundred dollar bills. "Here's five thousand," he said putting a rubber band around the money. "That should convince Dworkin you're serious. Text me after you've met." I put the money in my ugly purse.

"On second thought," Rabbi Goldberg added. "That wig looks horrible. Here's an extra five hundred dollars for a new one."

I took the extra money and turned to leave.

Rabbi Goldberg called after me, "You sure you don't want a crab cake to nosh on?"

"No thanks. I never eat *trafe* foods on the job."

10 A *Burqa* for Your Thoughts

I called the number Rabbi Goldberg had given me for Rabbi Dworkin. On the first ring, a man with a gruff Russian accent answered.

"Vat you vant?

"I want to meet Rabbi Dworkin. I'm having a medical problem and need a spare part."

"Who ees dees?"

"My name is Ruth Moscowitz. Is this Rabbi Dworkin?"

"My name Yuri. I verk vid Rabbi. Meet Saturday night at Mazel Tov Kosher Pizza, ten pm. Don't be late or no spare part. Vat you look like?"

"You'll recognize me. I've got a red scarf."

Wearing a red scarf was lame, but it would have to do. But how else would I distinguish myself from other Orthodox women in that restaurant?

Later that night, I sat across the kitchen table drinking a can of Natty Boh and chewing my nails. I'd told Don just enough about my new case to get his cop antenna buzzing.

"I think you're walking into a trap," Don warned in between chews of pizza. "Both rabbis smell like perps to me," he continued. "Yuri could be an enforcer for the Russian mob—they control most kosher restaurants in Westwood. Want me to call in a favor and have an unmarked car tail you? I'm getting worried I may never see you again."

Don had never offered to call in a favor for me before, it was against the rules and he always followed the letter of the law.

"I can handle those clowns," I said, reaching for a slice with extra anchovies. "I've dealt with worse."

I put on a brave face, but I wasn't fooling Don. I hated going into situations where I was out numbered, and possibly outgunned. I probably did need back up. But who? If only Archie could carry a weapon.

My mind filled with more questions. Who could I get on short notice to dress up like an Orthodox Jew? Could they handle themselves if the situation went sideways? Would they need a gun?

A lightbulb clicked on in my head: Jerome! He's perfect. A transexual bail bondsman could surely come in handy to a girl in a bind.

Jerome and I met when Lenny was accused for killing the boy in the dog park. After Lenny's name was cleared and the real killer was locked up, Jerome and I became friends. I liked him, and on a practical basis, as a bail bondsman he could legally run license plate numbers and enter someone's home without a warrant. And he packed a

Glock pistol, pepper spray, and a set of pink handcuffs.

I texted Jerome. He arrived like a genie flying out of a magic lamp. Within an hour, his six-foot-three-inch frame was perched on the edge of my couch. He delicately filed his nails and puffed away the filings.

"Sounds like a fine mess of a case you've gotten yourself involved with," he said, pointing a hot pink nail file at me.

"I'm happy to be your wingwoman for this rendezvous, but I generally steer clear of religion. The bible doesn't mention drag queens, an unforgivable sin of omission."

"Get out of your trannyverse, Jerome. It's a big world out there. Besides, this gig pays well. Are you in?"

"Honey, I never say no to dressing up, even for a religious masquerade. I think I can manage to throw together a hip and holy outfit that will wow your Rabbi and his Russian boy toy."

"Please don't get carried away," I said. "The assignment is to dress like an Orthodox woman, not like you're in a John Waters movie. No leopard prints. No beehive bubble wigs. Can you manage that?"

He winked a mascaraed eye at me. "Have a little faith."

Two hours later, I left Mt. Jefferson for the short ride to the rendezvous. I glanced in my rearview mirror. I was being tailed. For a second I thought it might be one of Don's buddies, but the car was too much of a junker for an undercover cop. Who was following me? I hit the brakes and came to a screeching halt. Instead of hitting me, the driver zoomed around and sped off. I had just enough time to pull a partial Maryland license plate number. I made a mental note to have Jerome run the plate.

I pulled into Mazel Tov Kosher Pizza's parking lot. Orthodox families were streaming toward the brightly lit eatery. I breathed a sigh of relief, the more people, the less likely an ambush. Jerome and I had agreed to meet early. I hoped he had dressed conservatively, but doubted he could resist the lure of wearing too much blue eye shadow or putting on a padded bra. I knew how he loved to show off his fake boobs. Drag queen habits are hard to break.

Someone rapped on my window. I gasped. Jerome stood with his hands clasped together as if in prayer. He was swaddled from head to toe in a dark blue robe. On his head was a foot-tall white turban and his eyes were outlined in dark khol. Green sparkly loops dangled from his ears.

"Get your butt outta the car," he mouthed through the glass. "I need you to give me the once over before our meeting with your Rabbi and his mobster rent boy."

I stepped out of the car. "I told you to dress conservatively, not to wear a damn *burqa*! Didn't you look at the pictures I emailed to you? You can't go into a kosher restaurant looking like Cleopatra!"

Jerome put his hands on his hips. "This is the best I can do on short notice. It's an *abaya*, not a *burqa*. I borrowed it from a Muslim friend. And another thing Miss Know-It-All, Orthodox Jewish women and Muslim women obey the same rules of modesty. So zip it"

I held the restaurant door open as Jerome wiggled his hips and butt like a fashion model striding down a runway. I counted to ten and hoped for the best.

Dog Spelled Backwards

11 Meeting Dworkin

Jerome sashayed through the restaurant like he owned the place. His towering frame, ridiculours dress, and over the top eyeliner caused a hush to fall over the room. As I walked behind this gargantuan drag queen, I held my head high and tried to act normal. In comparison to Jerome, my own outfit—an oversized sweater, long brown skirt and itchy, page boy wig— helped me blend in with the crowd.

I followed Jerome past the tables laden with *gefilte* fish and cheese *blintzes* to find Rabbi Dworkin and Yuri sitting at a booth near the rest rooms. My stomach clutched when I spied Yuri. He appeared as I had imagined: three hundred pounds of steroid-injected Soviet-born gangster with a shaved head and a meaty neck . He curled his lip to reveal two gold teeth.

I was about to extend my hand to Rabbi Dworkin then quickly let it drop to my side. One breach Orthodox etiquette and would give me away. I hoped that Jerome wouldn't make the same mistake.

"You vill sit please," Yuri said pointing to the vacant banquette across from Rabbi Dworkin. A waiter placed four mugs of hot tea front of us.

"You vill drink now," demanded Yuri. I took a sip of steaming tea, burnt my tongue, and gagged. As I reached for a glass of ice water, Jerome winked coquettishly at Yuri, slowly licking at the lipstick on his puckered, cherry-red lips. I kicked him hard under the table.

"Well now, Miss Moscowitz," said the Rabbi, stroking his bushy white beard. "I wasn't aware you would be bringing your..." he raised his eyebrows, "sister?"

"She's not my sister," I deflected. "This is my aunt...Aunt Ziporah. She's from India."

"Splendid!" said Rabbi Dworkin, clapping his chubby hands. "There are so few Jews left in India. Surely your aunt knows Isaac Sarmad's family. I visited the New Delhi synagogue last year. Tell me," he said nodding at Jerome, "how is Isaac?"

Before I could give Jerome another kick, he blurted in a falsetto voice, "Isaac and Sarah send you their blessings. They hope you'll celebrate Passover with them." I exhaled with relief. Jerome was good at thinking on his feet, maybe the Rabbi and Yuri would ignore his outrageous outfit.

The Rabbi smiled broadly at Jerome, and Yuri cracked a smile, his gold teeth glinting under the fluorescent lights. Jerome had passed the test.

"I hope you're hungry Miss Moscowitz," said Dworkin, handing me a plastic menu. "Eat first then we'll talk about kidneys."

I kept one eye on the menu and one on Dworkin. He didn't give off a creepy vibe like Rabbi Goldberg. Still, he trafficked in black market body parts and his bodyguard acted like a sociopath with an eighth grade education. I didn't know much about rabbis, but I was pretty sure not all of them were this sketchy.

"The falafal sandwich and potato knish are good," said Rabbi Dworkin, pointing to me and then to the menu. "But you should choose the *babaganoush*."

I had no idea what the Rabbi was recommending, but I ordered it anyway. "I'm sure the *babaganoush* will be delicious," I said, patting my flat stomach, hoping it wouldn't make me retch.

Jerome piped in. "My mother, may she rest in peace, made the best *babaganoush* in India. She couldn't walk down the street without people stopping to ask for the recipe. Mine is just as irresistable."

"Vill you make me *babaganoush* soon?" asked Yuri. "I not working tomorrow. We make date for *babaganoush*, yes?"

"Let me check my calendar first, but I'm sure I could squeeze you in," said Jerome. I kicked him again. "Please excuse us," I muttered. "We need to go to the ladies' room." I grabbed Jerome's elbow and dragged him to an alcove near the rest rooms.

"*Babaganoush*? I hissed. You don't even know what it is. And a date with that Terminator wanna be? I thought you were a professional. If you blow this job hiding the salami with Yuri, I am going to...."

Just then, the men's room door opened and Lenny walked out.

"Shit," I muttered.

"Hi Jane," said Lenny, barely able to control his glee. "Is that you Jerome? I hardly recognized you. I had no idea you kept kosher."

"No more stupid questions!" I hollered to Lenny. "Jerome and I are working. Why are *you* here?"

Lenny beamed. "Meet my future wife!" He pointed to a petite woman, with honey-colored hair in a blue dress, waving demurely from table against the wall.

"That's Sarah. Isn't she beautiful?" gushed Lenny. "Sarah is Rabbi Goldberg's niece. He played matchmaker for us. This is our fifth date, so now we're officially engaged and I'm going to ask her the big question tonight. I'm so nervous I almost left the ring at home."

"You're getting married after just five dates? What's the matter with you?"

"Mazel tov, Lenny," said Jerome, waving and blowing the woman a kiss. "She's a pretty little thing, but if you don't mind my saying, that dress does nothing for her lovely figure. And that hairstyle, it's so 1986! She needs Miss Jerome to give her my famous make over."

"Everybody knock it off," I said. "Lenny, Jerome and I are happy for you, but we've got work to do. Go! Scram!"

Lenny hustled back to his table while Jerome craned his neck and smiled at Yuri. I squeezed Jerome's arm. "Can you please keep your libido in check and behave like the professional transsexual bail bondsman I hired?"

Dog Spelled Backwards

"Yuri," Jerome sighed. "He's one hottie. Eastern European too. I haven't had a man like that in a long, long time. But friendship is more important than my sorry ass love life. For you, I'll back off and get down to business."

"Thanks. Now let's get back to our table before they get suspicious."

Jerome and I sat down just as the food arrived. I was about to dig in when Rabbi Dworkin cleared his throat. "We need to say the blessings before the meal." He mumbled a prayer in Hebrew. "*Essen,* eat and enjoy," said Dworkin, gobbling a piece of bread.

Yuri shoveled a mound of *babaganoush* in his mouth. I stared at lumpy gray concoction and tried to figure out if it was animal, mineral or vegetable.

"What, you don't like eggplant spread?" Rabbi Dworkin said. I bravely sampled a forkful. It was slimy and tasted of garlic and olive oil. At that moment I would have sold my soul for a cheeseburger.

I couldn't wait for the meal to be over so we could get down to business. When the last plate was finally cleared, Rabbi Dworkin shook out his napkin and delicately wiped away bits of food from his beard. He leaned toward me and adjusted his wire-rimmed glasses.

"So, you have advanced polycystic kidney disease?" he asked in a sing-song manner. "I'm told you won't go through the standard channels to get your kidney."

I nodded dumbly.

"Shall I assume you can't get a kidney from a relative or friend?" He glanced quizzically at Jerome. "I usually guarantee a kidney from a live donor in the United States. While it's always better for the patient to receive a kidney from a living person, there is always the option of harvesting a kidney from a cadaver. This non-consensual route is what I suggest for budget conscious clients. But I'd never traffic in kidneys from the Third World. No, not me, that's unethical."

Dog Spelled Backwards

I shuddered to think of someone carving a kidney out of a corpse, then sewing the cold organ into a living person.

"As I was saying," said Dworkin, "you have two options: live donor or cadaver kidney. I'd pick the live option. The kidney will last longer and I offer a five-year guarantee. If your replacement kidney fails, you get a new kidney at a deep discount. I am a man of my word and a man of God. I promise you a quality kidney at a good price so you should live a long and healthy life."

"How much will my quality kidney cost?" I asked in a weak voice. I'd better get used to acting like I was dying if I was going to convince anyone that I was desperately in need of a major body part.

"To a nice lady like you fifty-thousand dollars for the down payment. The day of the operation you give me another fifty-thousand. Total one hundred thousand— cash of course. Yuri will make sure your money is safe." Yuri rubbed his fore finger and thumb together.

My mind was whirring like a hard drive about to crash. One hundred-thousand cash for a kidney? No wonder Rabbi Goldberg was so interested in finding out the particulars of Dworkin's operation. This scam was a renal goldmine.

"I can get you the money," I said, thinking of Rabbi Goldberg's cash.

"Not to worry. You'll need to see one of my doctors for a check up first to make sure you're good for a transplant. I don't sell just anyone a kidney; my clients need to be healthy, and trustworthy. I don't want any problems with the police." He nodded at Yuri. "Yuri makes sure everyone is one hundred percent kosher."

I gulped. I needed to see a doctor? There's nothing wrong with my kidneys. This was major wrench in the machinery. I thought fast...I'd need to get some fake blood tests and forge medical reports. It would take some doing, but I could pull it off.

"I'll make an appointment," I said confidently.

"See Dr. Kornblatt. I'll cover his cost as a gesture of good will. But make the appointment soon so we can get you a beautiful new kidney."

Rabbi Dworkin stood up. "*Gezai gezunt*, be well. I'll speak after your examination."

Yuri grinned at Jerome. "You give me phone number. I call."

Jerome batted his fake eyelashes. "A lady never gives out her number."

"No problem," Yuri laughed. "You not real lady."

12 Welcome to My Nightmare

I lay on a stainless steel table in a sterile operating room, a ball gag in my mouth stifling my frantic cries. Blinding lights illuminated my naked body. I felt like a piece of meat awaiting the butcher's cleaver.

I thrashed side-to-side, leather cuffs tearing jigsaw cuts into my ankles and wrist. I pounded my bound fists against the table. A gloved hand gripped a shining scalpel. It moved close to my chest. Tears streamed from the corners of my eyes and into my ears. The edge of the scalpel pressed against my throat. I held my breath as the blade ripped a bloody furrow into my flesh from my breastbone to my navel. Molten pain seared my chest before everything turned black.

Don held me, his heart beating wildly against my chest. "Are you having a nightmare? You've been kicking me for the last five minutes." Archie crouched next to me thumping his tail, his head cocked and worried.

I raked my fingers through my sweaty hair and exhaled through my mouth. I patted my chest just to make sure it had all been a bad dream. A tough chick like me doesn't need job anxieties or bad dreams about freaks pulling body parts out of people against their will.

Don furrowed his brow. "If you're not gonna tell me about your nightmare, how about if I make breakfast, eggs and corned beef hash?"

The thought of food gave me the dry heaves. My gut pulsed waves of nausea. I needed to kick something to exorcise the demons from my rattled brain.

I slid out of bed and into my sports bra and sweat pants. Archie followed me down the wooden stairs into the condo's basement, Don's man cave and my home boxing gym. I started my warm up by jumping rope for five minutes. I needed a hard workout to steel myself for today's appointment with Dr. Kornblatt.

I slipped my engagement ring off and put in on the coffee table before tugging on red leather boxing gloves. After touching my toes and cracking my neck, it was time to start my boxing drills. I threw quick, right-handed jabs, then cross punches against the eighty-pound heavy bag.

The muffled thwack of my gloves against the leather bag soothed me. The harder I smacked the heavy bag, the faster my dark mood lifted. I bobbed and weaved around the room. Archie chased me into a corner, playfully barking and snarling. "You think you got me on the ropes, sucker!" I feigned jabs and hooks then threw in some quick uppercuts.

When I could barely lift my arms, I dropped to the floor and counted out a

Dog Spelled Backwards

hundred crunches, my stomach muscles taught as the sheets on a newly made bed.

I took off my gloves, the heavy bag still swaying from my punching drills. My hands ached and my knees shook from fatigue and low blood sugar. I sucked my bleeding knuckles while Archie nipped at my pants.

"Help with my warm down," I said to Archie. We jogged in tight circles around the room for a minute before collapsing on the couch. "Whose's my tough guy?" I said, putting him in a headlock. "If anyone comes after me you bite first, I'll ask questions later."

After a quick shower, it was time to visit Dr. Kornblatt and be evaluated for my black market kidney. A folder medical records stating that I was suffering from end-stage renal disease and in need on an immediate kidney transplant was stuffed into my handbag.

It wasn't easy creating these phony documents. In the past week I'd stayed up all night reading academic papers and medical textbooks on kidney function and types of kidney disease.

Once I was up to speed, I created a medical dossier with falsified blood and urine tests. According to my bogus medical records, my symptoms began a year ago with blood in my urine and back pain. These fake tests, ordered by an equally fake Dr. Hector Camacho; an homage to my favorite boxer, showed that I had dangerously high levels of creatinine and blood urea nitrogen along with elevated serum albumin and anti-nuclear anti-bodies. In layperson's terms, my kidneys were shot.

To bolster my story that I couldn't get a kidney through legitimate channels, I printed out a chain of fake emails from the Maryland Kidney Network. The emails detailed that I was number three hundred fifty-nine on the waiting list for a new kidney. That meant I could be on dialysis for two years before a new kidney might become available. By the time I'd completed my research and compiled my phony medical records, I nearly convinced myself I had kidney disease.

Order a pizza, I'll be home by six, I texted Don before beginning my drive to Westwood. I turned left onto Reisterstown Road passing Rosenzweig's Used Cars and Uncle John's Lake Trout before parking my Toyota in front of a ramshackle brick house row house.

The house was a wreck: broken windows, a week-choked lawn and a front porch that looked like it was about to cave in. This couldn't be Dr. Kornblatt's office, I thought, unless he worked out of a crack den. I had to be at the wrong address. What kind of doctor would practice in a dump like this?

A woman holding a baby tapped my shoulder. "Your first time seeing Dr. Kornblatt?" she said with a knowing smile. I nodded. "Everyone's scared at first. But It'll all work out."

She led me around an obstacle course of overflowing trash cans, bald tires and unidentifiable junk to the back of the house. In the urine-stained yard a howling white dog was chained to a post. The poor thing was skinny as a broomstick.

I squatted down and stroked its boney flank as it whimpered and shivered. I looked closer. It was a bull terrier, just like Archie! My heart clutched. I wished I had some dog treats to offer. "Hang in there, buddy" I said softly.

The dog rubbed its muzzle against my hand. "I promise I'll come back to rescue you."

Dog Spelled Backwards

13 To Save a Life

I followed the woman down a crumbling flight of stairs that led to Dr. Kornblatt's waiting area. The acidic stink of urine assaulted my nostrils as I entered the shabby room. Overhead, fluorescent lights flickered and buzzed and cast a sickly pallor over the moaning men and women hunched over on folding chairs.

Among the sick, dying and desperate people around me, I stood out like a turd in a punchbowl. In spite of the layers of ghostly-pale make up I'd slathered on my face, I still looked a million times healthier than anyone in the room. An old man with sunken cheeks lifted his rheumy eyes and gestured for me to sit beside him. He clapped his boney hand on top of mine, a single tear escaped from his bloodshot eye. "I don't want to die," he croaked. I wanted to feel sorry for him but I was creeped out by the engorged ostomy bag affixed to his waist.

Squeezing my hand, he intoned: "all of my doctors tell me I'm too old for a transplant, and since I'm dying from diabetes anyway, what's the point of throwing away a good kidney?" More tears escaped from his cloudy eyes. "Dr. Kornblatt won't turn me away. *Shayna maidela,* you are in the prime of your life, he'll save you. Young or old, Dr. Kornblatt knows that life is precious." I tried pulling my hand away, but he gripped it like a corpse trying to drag the living into the next world.

A woman in a rusty wheelchair rolled up. "He's right, it's the law of *Pekuach nefesh*—the Torah's injunction for us to preserve life at all costs," she said. Hanging from her sinewy neck was a Star of David. She rubbed it between her fingers like it was a talisman. I cringed at the crone, she reminded me of of witch. "Dr. Kornblatt gives hope to the dying," the woman

Dog Spelled Backwards

wheezed. "He's a holy man carrying out God's work."

The old man pointed to the woman who'd led me into Dr. Kornblatt's office. The mother cradled her sleeping infant in her arms, a beatific smile graced her placid face. The old man's eyes misted with emotion. "Look at that woman. She's only go six months to live," he said. "If she hadn't come to Dr. Kornblatt for help, that poor baby wouldn't have a mother. God knows what would happen to that child."

The old man's watery eyes seemed to look through me. My stomach knotted. Did he suspect I was a phony? I couldn't help but stare at the woman and her child. As I did, a powerful memory seized me. It bubbled up from the tarry depths of my childhood. My head spun. I was dragged back in time, transported to Sunday morning mass at St. Wojciech's. The heady aroma of frankincense and sandalwood filled my nostrils. I knelt in prayer, my knees pressed against the cold tile floor. Above me the choir sang a heart tugging version of *Serdeczna Matko*, the unofficial anthem of Poland. The woman and child in the dingy waiting room morphed into the Madonna and Child, symbols of unconditional love and faith that as a child I wanted so much to believe in. *Serdeczna matko, opiekunko ludzi... Beloved mother*, the choir mournfully chanted, *have compassion on the cries of the orphans: Eve's banished children, we implore you to care for us. Do not let us wander.*

A high pitched voice interrupted. "Miss Ruth Moscowitz, the doctor will see you in his office," a chubby woman in pink scrubs called out. I shook my hand to release it from the old man's death grip and walked through the door.

Dr. Kornblatt motioned for me to sit down in a stiff metal chair across from his desk. He was thin and clean shaven, dressed in a stylish blue suit with a striped tie. Framed pictures of the doctor with his smiling wife and children were arrayed around his neat desk. A diploma from The University of Maryland School of Medicine hung on the wall.

"I've reviewed your tests," he said fanning papers out on the desk. He looked directly at me. "What impresses me most is how well you've forged your laboratory results and confidential patient records," he said, tapping the papers. "You've even managed to steal someone's X-rays. That can't have been easy. I've never come across a healthy person who wants a kidney transplant. Do you have some kind of operation fetish?"

Shit, Kornblatt had blown my carefully constructed plan. My face flushed hot and my layers of make-up started to melt. Sweat trickled down by back. I needed to think fast now that plan A was trashed.

"Are you working for the police or Goldberg?" Kornblatt asked as I fidgeted and schemed. "Either way, I want you to hear your story. So which is it Miss Moscowitz, or whatever your real name is?"

"I'm not the police," I fessed up. "Goldberg is paying me to feed him details on your kidney scam. That's the truth." I crossed my arms. "Now it's my turn to ask you questions. This place isn't exactly Johns Hopkins Hospital. It's a shit hole. Why are you doing this?"

Kornblatt smiled patiently. "You've seen how sick and desperate my patients are. As a Jew, you know the expression *l'chaim*—to life? I'm not God, and it's not for to me to decide who will live or die. But if I can save one life, I have saved the whole world. That's why I perform kidney transplants. Everyone should have a chance to live."

In spite of Dr. Kornblatt's impassioned speech, my bullshit detector was ringing loud and clear. Thoughts clicked through my head: the shitty office, the pictures of Kornblatt's family, Kornblatt suspecting I was a cop. Click. Click. Click. In a flash, the whole picture came into focus. I pulled the hated wig off and rolled up my sleeves. I balled my fists, spitting mad at Kornblatt and everyone else who was jerking my chain. If I was being played by both Rabbis and a dirty doctor, heads were going to roll.

"Which Rabbi has you by the balls?" I growled. "Do you owe Goldberg money? Is Dworkin threatening your family unless you do these hack operations?"

Now it was Kornblatt's turn to sweat. I continued my interrogation.

Dog Spelled Backwards

"I see a diploma on the wall. Where did you get it, Kinkos? And while we're on the subject of bullshit, do you even know what a freaking kidney is?"

Kornblatt paced around his office. "Sit down!" I ordered, "I want the straight story. Any more lies and I'll beat the crap out of you."

He wrung his hands and looked down. "You got most of it right," he said, hanging his head. "I lost my medical license after a five-year-old girl died. I botched her surgery. But I don't remember what happened because I was skunk drunk."

"I'm an alcoholic, my whole life has been one drink after another. Dworkin helped me get sober, paid for my rehab and hired a team of top notch lawyers to fight a manslaughter charge. They got me acquitted but I lost my medical license. Without Dworkin's help, I'd be in jail and my wife would have divorced me."

"Keep going, Kornblatt. I'm crying a river."

"When Dworkin told me about his underground kidney procurement practice, I balked. But I needed to support my family. No one is going to hire an unlicensed doctor, so I agreed to help him."

"That's some story. Now tell me the parts you're leaving out."

Kornblatt shrugged. "That's everything."

I slammed my hands on his desk and shoved my face inches from his. His aftershave mixed with sweat stunk. "I swear I'll snap every one of your fingers until you tell me the whole truth."

I grabbed his arm and twisted his wrist. I bent his fingers back until I heard a pop. Kornblatt jerked like a fish on a line.

"Hey, that hurts!" he screamed. "Stop and I'll tell you more about Goldberg."

"Goldberg! What about him?" I let his arm drop.

"Goldberg has been trying to take over Dworkin's operation. This office is a gold mine. Dworkin accepts cash payments, hundreds of thousands of dollars flow through here every month. I've heard rumors about offshore bank accounts in the Cayman Islands. All I know is that Yuri the Russian comes by every Friday afternoon to collect the money." Kornblatt gestured toward a large safe in the corner.

My head spun. Yuri was working for Rabbi Goldberg! This was crazier, and more dangerous than I imagined.

"Where do you get the kidneys?"

Kornblatt blanched. "They, they, come from donors."

"Willing donors?" I asked, picturing people waking up in bathtubs of ice after a hard night of drinking minus their wallets and selected vital organs.

"Don't be so naive. Of course people are willing to donate their kidneys. People will do anything for cash. Believe me, it's not hard to find people hard up for money in Baltimore."

"Keep talking. How does Dworkin find these people?"

"He puts ads in craigslist and people flock to him to give up a healthy kidney for twenty five hundred dollars, no questions asked."

"Do you extract the kidneys?" I asked, my mind still fixated on the images of bloody bathtubs and dismembered organs.

"You offend me," Kornblatt said, holding his hand over his heart. "I only operate in Westwood, and on my own people. Goldberg has another doctor on his payroll. I hear he works out of a funeral parlor in East Baltimore on North Avenue near Greenmount Cemetery. And if God forbid, the operation fails and the person dies," Kornblatt winked. "The undertaker is right there to clean up the mess."

You've got to admire Goldberg's ingenuity, I thought. The man had accounted for every last detail.

"You got anything else you want to tell me, Kornblatt?"

"You seem like a smart woman, so I'm sure you've already figured out that the only reason Goldberg hired you was to cull every last detail about Dworkin."

I nodded. "Yeah, I kinda got that message loud and clear."

"Here's something you don't know; Goldberg is paying me a hundred grand to poison Dworkin."

My eyes widened. I wasn't sure I could keep track of who was screwing who.

"What?" was all I could say.

Kornblatt continued. "I've cultured botulinum toxin, the perfect poison, it's tasteless, odorless. Less than a milligram kills in an hour. I'll slip some into Dworkin's food when he stops by the office on Friday with Yuri to eat lunch and pick up the money. I won't be suspected. People die of botulism poisoning all the time."

Alarm bells were going off in my head. My mind quickly formed a mental diagram of who was going down: Kornblatt poisons Dworkin so Goldberg can take over the black market kidney operation. Goldberg hires me to supposedly get the goods on Dworkin, who's using me to get the details of the operation. Goldberg probably doesn't trust Kornblatt not to poison him too. I gulped. I was the weakest link in this knotted chain. After today's parlay with Kornblatt, I knew too much for either Goldberg or Dworkin to keep me around much longer. Fuck. I was number one on both rabbi's hit lists!

Kornblatt must have read my mind. "If I were you, I'd get far away from Westwood, maybe even leave the country. As a Jew, the Right of Return Law allows you to immigrate to Israel, no questions asked."

I didn't have the time to explain to Kornblatt that I wasn't sure if I was Jewish enough. Still, Kornblatt was right, I did need to get the hell out of his office.

"Use the back door," Kornblatt said. "You never know when Yuri will visit."

"Sorry I hurt you," I said, gathering my wig and fake records. Kornblatt nursed his wrist like a child holding a bird with a broken wing. "I'm a doctor. I can fix it," he said in a clinical voice. He nodded toward his waiting room. "You need to leave fast."

He slid open the deadbolt of the door leading to the back of his office.

I exited into the back yard. In the middle of the broken concrete sat the dog. It wagged its tail and yipped as I bent down to pet its head. "Let's get you outta this hell hole." I unhooked the pitiful creature from the rusted chain. "Hey little egghead," I cooed as the dog's black and pink nose twitched. The bull terrier snuggled its muzzle into my neck and licked my ear. I lifted its skinny body into my arms and carried the shivering dog to my car.

"To save a life," I said softly to the dog. "To save a life."

14 All About Eve

The bull terrier was fast asleep, snoring peacefully in the passenger seat during the short drive to Mt. Jefferson. I pulled into the Dunkin Donuts drive through window and ordered and extra large black coffee.

Up for a big surprise? I texted Don.

You're pregnant? he texted back.

Pregnant! I was too busy trying to deal with the double crossing rabbis to worry about making babies.

I couldn't hear myself think as I walked into the living room with the sleeping dog in my arms. The volume on the big screen television was turned up so loud the beer bottles on the coffee table vibrated like a small earthquake was hitting our condo. Don was sprawled on the couch in his Raven's football jersey, idly scratching his balls, his glassy-eyed glaze fixed on the football game. Next to him, Lenny snoozed, a half-eaten sandwich in his lap.

I put the new dog on the floor. It ran behind my legs. I grabbed the remote and turned off the television. Don sat up with a look of horror in his face. "Uh oh, Mama's home," he said blushing.

"Wake up Lenny," I called out. Lenny slowly shook himself awake like Rip Van Winkle after his twenty-year slumber. Then he resumed eating.

I cleared my throat. "Now that I've got everyone's attention. I'd like to introduce you to the newest member of the family."

At the sound of my voice, Archie thundered down the stairs, sprinting into the living room at top speed before coming to a screeching halt at my feet. His moist nose twitched from side to side, no doubt scenting the creature hiding behind me. The dog peeked its head in between my legs and surveyed the room, its ebony-colored triangular eyes meeting Archie's. Both dogs held each other's gaze like a they were linked in a doggie tractor beam.

I tried to coax the dog out from between my legs but it was too frightened to move. I knew what would motivate the dog.

"Lenny, get me some cheese, the stinkier the better." Lenny extracted a tub of blue cheese from the refrigerator. I took a bit in my hand and coaxed the dog out from behind me. The dog sniffed the pungent morsel then gulped it. Archie sat on his haunches, his enormous head at the same level as the new dog. Tentatively, the dogs touched noses. Then Archie licked the other dog's face. The new dog rolled submissively onto its back. Archie sniffed the dog's crotch then began playfully licking its bat-like ears.

Lenny smiled. "Archie has a girlfriend."

Don kissed me and pinched my bottom. "Now you're not the only bitch in the house, Janey."

I rolled my eyes and put my hands on my bony hips. "Let's get one thing straight, I'll always be top bitch around here. End of story."

Lenny scratched the new dog's ears. It growled contentedly. "Where did you get this little sweetie? Did you steal her?"

"Technically, yes," I conceded. "If you consider rescuing a starving dog that was probably chained up in a filthy concrete prison yard her whole life stealing then yes, I am guilty as charged. You got a problem with that?"

"No Jane," Lenny backpedaled. "I think God will forgive you in this case."

"You're like the Marines, Janey: *no dog left behind,*" Don said, opening a bottle of beer with his teeth and spitting the bottle cap onto the carpet. "What are we gonna call this little girl?"

"I have a suggestion," Lenny volunteered, adjusting his *yarmulke*. "Let's call her Eve. The Torah says that after God created Adam, he declared 'it is not good for man to be alone; I will make him a helper.' Archie and

Eve, a fitting homage to the first woman in the bible, don't you think?"

"Once in a blue moon, a good idea escapes from that thick skull of yours, cousin," I said. Lenny blushed at my left-handed compliment. Eve trailed after Archie as he walked a circuit around the living room, peeing first against the couch and then the leg of the dining room table.

"They're just marking their territory," Lenny said evenly as Eve squatted and pooped on the carpet.

"You," I said, pointing at Don who was ready to escape, beer in hand to his man cave, "get some Lysol." I tossed Lenny a roll of paper towels. "Help Don clean up."

"Yes ma'am," Don mock saluted. Lenny hummed and blotted the carpet with paper towels. Across the room, Archie and Eve were snuggled against each other. For a minute, everything was peaceful in the house.

Dog Spelled Backwards

15 The Root of All Evil

With Don and the dogs sprawled across the king-sized mattress, and only a sliver of mattress available, I was the odd creature out for tonight's sleeping arrangements. If there was any hope of getting a few hours of rest, I'd need to either sleep on the couch or Archie's dog bed.

I sat cross-legged on the battered couch, the scratchy afghan wrapped around my shoulders against the cold. From the kitchen, the tea kettle whistled. Biting my gnawed nails, I reviewed the events of the last few days. Here's what I knew: I was caught in the middle of an unholy mess.

Rabbis Goldberg and Dworkin professed to be holy men but were hiding behind their *yarmulkes* while up to their eyeballs in illegal activities.

Framing the situation in biblical terms: Rabbi Goldberg coveted Rabbi Dworkin's black market kidney operation; an enterprise that raked in hundreds of thousands of dollars a year, money that sick people begged borrowed or maybe stole with the hope they could prolong their lives.

Kornblatt was a defrocked doctor who regarded himself as an angel of mercy for performing illegal, back alley kidney surgeries. Where he got his kidneys from, I still had no idea, but I was dead sure he wasn't ordering them from kidneys.com.

Kornblatt was being blackmailed by Dworkin, who had Kornblatt performing illegal operations in return for bailing out his family. To get himself out from under Dworkin's thumb, Kornblatt was secretly working for Goldberg and was about to poison Dworkin. Once Dworkin was out of the picture, Goldberg would be the kidney king of Westwood. Meanwhile, Yuri, the

Dog Spelled Backwards

Russian muscle, was playing all sides; working for both rabbis to see which one would come out on top.

An ice pick stabbed my temple and my eye watered. A tingling Aurora Borealis of colors and shapes blurred my vision. I retched as a tsunami of a migraine crashed over me. I poured a cup of tea and swallowed a double dose of migraine medicine. Massaging the braided knots at the base of my skull, I winced as the diamond on my engagement ring dug into the nape of my neck, a sharp reminder of my upcoming wedding. If I didn't dig myself out of this quagmire, there wasn't going to be a wedding.

A flushing sound from the bedroom told me that Don had gotten up to pee. I hoped he'd remembered to put the toilet seat down. It was bad enough that Archie drank out of the toilet, I didn't want Eve picking up that bad habit. Archie padded into the living room. "I'm having a pity party. Want to join me?" I said to Archie as he climbed into my lap.

Everything was going to shit. Anger and frustration oozed from every pore. Searching for someone to blame, Lenny's moon-shaped face appeared like a thought bubble over my aching head. My damn cousin always managed to lead me into a lion's den of problems. I cursed Lenny for introducing me to Rabbi Goldberg. Yeah, he probably thought he was doing me a favor, but in typical Lenny style, none of his good deeds ever went unpunished. I'd already helped Lenny beat a murder rap, and I could count on both both hands the times I got him out of hot water when we were kids. Some people have a God-given talent for screwing up other people's lives, and in this arena, Lenny was triply blessed.

I fumed as I plotted how I was going punish Lenny. But as mad as I was with Lenny, and as much as I wanted to kick his ass, deep down I had to face the truth: I was responsible for my problems. We weren't kids anymore. I was a grown woman fully capable of creating and solving my own problems. The more I thought about it, the clearer the answer

Dog Spelled Backwards

became: money was the root of most of my problems. I'd been greedy for a quick fix of cash and hungrily reached for what I thought was easy money dispensed from a man that my gut told me was crooked. If I hadn't been so damn obsessed with money, I never wouldn't have taken the job with Rabbi Goldberg.

I lay on the couch with eyes closed, the headache pounding my head like a chorus line of sadistic tap dancers. It wouldn't take years of expensive psychoanalysis to discover why I was such an angry bitch. The answers were almost stereotypically banal. Since I was little, I resented being the poor kid in a Mt. Jefferson, a neighborhood made up of haves and have-nots. This Third World distribution of wealth gnawed at my soul. In Mt. Jefferson I was made to feel like a stinking peasant in a kingdom of untold wealth.

Long buried memories of my mother came back to me. I hardly ever thought about my mother, it was too painful for me to dredge up the past. Still, I couldn't stop the flood of memories that now filled my mind. My mother worked two jobs and never allowed herself any luxuries. Her efforts left her a bitter and exhausted woman. I was convinced she was resentful of the opportunities I had as young woman in America. In the end, all of my mother's hard work and sacrifice took its toll. She died of pancreatic cancer when I was a senior in high school. By then I'd already done as much as I could to distance myself from her and to wall myself up from the outside world.

Maybe Lenny was right when he said I was having an identity crisis.

But wasn't I changing? I'd allowed someone to love me. Don wanted to take care of me. Hell, he wanted to marry me and knock me up. Throw in a white picket fence and season tickets to the Ravens and Orioles and Don's life would be complete. I was softening around the edges, that was for sure. But I couldn't tell if that was a good thing. And with Lenny's news of my mother's secret, that she was Jewish but hid her religion from me, even going as far as sending me to church for years, I was even more confused about who I was and what I should believe.

I flashed back to Bosco and Zodiac Detective Agency. It had scarcely been a month since I'd quit in a huff. I missed my old job. Yeah, Bosco was a sexist pig who gave me lousy assignments that paid crap, but at least he was honest—and most important, he wasn't trying to kill me.

My eyelids drooped and my neck muscles relaxed as the migraine dragon receded back into its headache cave. It was time to catch a few hours of sleep. I'd barely laid my head on the cushion when my iPhone buzzed with a text message. What asshole was texting me at this hour?

Heard about your meeting with Dr. Kornblatt. Good work! Meet me at 7pm tomorrow at my house & give me all the details. I've got $3,000 cash for you. Rabbi G.

Crap. I'd been dodging Rabbi Goldberg's calls and emails for the past three days. I couldn't avoid him much longer. I'd meet with Goldberg, take my money then run like hell.

C u then, I texted back.

16 When the Bullet Hits the Bone

I zipped up my black leather motorcycle jacket over hip hugging jeans and my beloved Judas Priest T-shirt. I reached to a high shelf in the bedroom closet and brushed a layer of dust off the locked metal box that held my tools of the trade. I popped the lock. *Hello, bad girl toys.*

I polished my trusty brass knuckles with the end of my T-shirt and tucked them into my back pocket. I checked the magazine on my high performance taser C2. The beast emitted thirty seconds of high powered juice that could drop a violent felon at fifteen paces.

Facing the bedroom mirror, I practiced firing the taser at Yuri, envisioning the look of agony on his face as five thousand volts of juice lit up his nervous system. I smiled evilly at the sight of Yuri peeing and shitting himself before dropping to the ground like a drunk. I kissed the taser then placed it in its tactical holster at my waist. What the hell, I thought as I grabbed a can of mace. You never know when you need to temporarily blind someone.

Meanwhile, Archie and Eve waged a gladiatorial tug-of-war with Don's jeans. Eve splayed her white paws and growled, digging her powerful teeth deeper into the denim, dragging Archie toward her. "You gonna let a girl beat you Archie?" I teased as Eve pulled Archie across the room. In a few minutes Don's jeans would be reduced to a tangle of rags.

A sliver of moon peeked through the bare trees as I drove into Westwood. After twenty minutes of circling the narrow side streets, I wedged my dented Toyota between two cargo vans. None of the street lights along the block were working. All I

Dog Spelled Backwards

had to illuminate my path to Rabbi Goldberg's house was the tiny flashlight on my keychain.

Someone coughed. "Who the fuck are you?" I called out as I wheeled around, shining my toy flashlight like a little kid on a sleepover. The weak beam captured the spooky outline of man. He scurried out of range behind a nearby house. Damn it. I couldn't believe how careless I'd gotten over the past few weeks. Not only had I forgotten to pack my police-strength flashlight, I'd neglected to have Jerome run the license plate of car that had tailed me to my meeting with Rabbi Dworkin. Now I was being followed again! I threw the Cracker Jack prize flashlight in the gutter and slapped my face. *Get a grip Jane.*

Rabbi Goldberg's house was dark as a tomb. I skirted the high hedge surrounding the house and stopped short of the stoop. I pulled my taser out of its holster, making sure the device was set to its maximum charge. An envelope with my name on it taped to the door. Looking right and left, I grabbed the envelope and tore it open. A wad of hundred dollar bills tumbled into my hand along with a note: *"Here is the money I owe you. You're terminated. Shalom, Rabbi Goldberg."*

Terminated. I didn't bother counting the money, I had to get the hell out of Westwood.

Before I could grab my car keys, I heard a rustle from behind a tree. I turned my head toward the sound. In the next second, a blast ripped through the night. My right hand reflexively touched a warm hole in my leather jacket. My left shoulder had taken a direct hit. A second bullet kamikazied into me. Blood dripped down my neck from the jagged edges of what was remained of my left ear. I started blacking out. Spasms of chills racked my body. I was going into shock.

A wave of pain hit me like I'd driven head first into a concrete wall. I bit my tongue to distract me from the fiery wound in my shoulder and the infernal wailing in my one good ear.

"*Control yourself, Jane*" I said through gritted teeth. I had to get myself to safety. Every second I waited was one step closer to my killers finishing me off and dumping my body into the filthy waters off Sparrow's Point. I had to get to my car.

Ignoring the pain, I dragged myself from the middle of the sidewalk, hunkering between the curb and a parked car. I nursed my shoulder. The blood on my neck was starting to dry. It cracked and flaked as I scanned for the shooter. I touched my left ear. It felt like fleshy shredded wheat.

I couldn't wait in the gutter until the police arrive or someone put a bullet in my skull. Jockeying into a sprinter's crouch, I readied myself to rocket across the street and run all the way to Reisterstown Road. With the street lights out I had a decent chance of zig zagging my way around the parked cars to throw off my pursuer.

Where were the cops? The gunshots were certain to attract someone's attention. Westwood wasn't the kind of neighborhood where gunplay was an everyday occurrence. Strange, no one had come out to of their homes to see what was going on. I reached for my iPhone to call 911, but it was gone. It must have fallen out when I ran down the sidewalk. I heard a mosquito-like buzz then a metallic crack as a bullet whizzed over my head hitting a car and setting off its alarm.

Wounds or no wounds, it was time to go. Holding my bad arm to my body, I ran unsteadily across the street. My legs felt like water balloons, my equilibrium gone thanks to the bullet that shattered my eardrum. I got as far as the other side of the street before collapsing again next to an oak tree.

The effort of crossing the street thoroughly exhausted me. I'd lost too much blood to run any farther. Sapped of all of my strength, and unable to use my weapons, I was dead meat. No guardian angel was going to reach down and swoop me out of this trap.

I didn't have enough energy to compile a full litany of my life's regrets, but I had to try. I wished I hadn't been such a bitch to Lenny and Don. That was wrong. My shoulder pounded. A fresh spurt of blood

Dog Spelled Backwards

ran down my shirt. I needed to say some kind of prayer, but I didn't know how. God didn't take mercy on people like me. I said goodbye to Don, then to Archie and Eve. Finally, I said goodbye to Lenny. I was going to miss that pain in the ass. I closed my eyes, ready for Yuri to put a bullet in my head and end it all.

The *whoop whoop* of a siren sounded in the distance. Opening my eyes, a line of yellow flickering lights headed toward me at top speed. A car screeched to a halt. I peeked my head from behind the tree expecting to see the Baltimore police coming at me with guns drawn.

But instead of cops, two burly men in reflective vests with Hebrew lettering jogged toward me, their walkie talkies squawking and bouncing against their hips.

A man with a raggedy beard knelt beside me. He spoke into his walkie talkie. "We've located the victim. She's alive, badly wounded." He turned to the second man. "Get an ambulance right away. The shooter is still at large. We need back up."

"Where were you shot?" he asked. I pointed to my ear and shoulder.

"You're Jewish police?" I croaked, eyeing their *yarmulkas*.

"Guess you're not from this neighborhood," the men chuckled. "We are *shomrim,* a Jewish civilian patrol that keeps Westwood safe," said the man with the beard. "Now you're our responsibility. We'll make sure you get to the hospital."

"Someone tried to kill me," I said, my good ear buzzing and clicking. "Shouldn't you call the *real* police?"

The men shot me sour looks. "We'll take care of this problem on our own, young lady," the first man answered. "We're the law in this neighborhood and believe me, the *shomrim* always get their man."

With the arrival of the first *shomrim,* house lights came on along both sides of the block. Families of curious Orthodox men, women and children tumbled out of their houses to see why the *shomrim* had been called. They pointed at me from the edge of their front lawns. I noticed that every house was lit up, except Rabbi Goldberg's.

More *shomrim* arrived. The men joined hands to form a perimeter around me, protecting me from the gawking neighbors.

A tier of red lights approached. Another siren wailed. "Here comes the *hatzalah*," one of the *shomrim* called out. "The paramedics will take it from here."

The men directed the vehicle through the scrum of onlookers. A shiny ambulance with blue and white Hebrew lettering pulled onto the lawn. A trio of Orthodox Jewish men hopped out of the ambulance and ran toward me with bulky medical bags. They unfolded a gurney and gently placed me on the white sheets then strapped me down.

"I'm starting an intravenous saline drip and adding a double dose morphine for your gunshot wounds," one of the attendants said to me. Another set of hands removed my leather jacket and peeled off my blood soaked T-shirt. I moaned as the attendant moved my shattered arm and started the IV. Within seconds all my pain dissolved.

"Who are you guys?" I said groggily.

"*Hatzalah*, the Jewish ambulance service," said the attendant. "We're taking you to Johns Hopkins Hospital. Is there anyone I can call to meet you there?"

"Call my fiancee Don Williams," I slurred. "Tell him I'm not dead."

Dog Spelled Backwards

17 A Woman of Valor

The doctor took off his thick surgical glasses and mopped his brow. "The operation was touch-and-go. We removed two bullets from her shoulder. There's a chance she may need more surgery if there are still bullet fragments. She's lost a lot of blood and some infection had set in. But she's very strong, and with extensive physical therapy she'll gain function back in her arm." He paused. "I've seen my share of scary tattoos in the operating room, but that giant tattoo on her back scared the life out of me."

Don snorted. "She's no gangster, doc, if that's what you're thinking. She's my fiancée. What caliber bullet?"

"Probably a 7.62 x 39 millimeter, most likely fired from an AK-47, possibly Russian made. But don't quote me on any of this. You'd better get your forensics team to confirm the ballistics."

"What about her ear?"

"The ear drum is destroyed so she's permanently deaf in her left ear. Even though she's lost a good portion of the outer ear, a good plastic surgeon will reconstruct it so she won't look like Mrs. Vincent van Gogh."

Don stepped closer to the doctor, lowering his voice. "Do they teach you that kind of humor in medical school? It's not funny."

"Sorry officer. I was out of line."

The hospital room was painted vomit yellow. I lay in a narrow bed, a hard pillow under my head. Everything inch of my body ached. Someone tugged my right arm. I swatted them away. I fought to wake up but kept falling back into my half-dreamland. Suddenly, my eyes popped open. "That hurts!" I slurred, spittle dripping from lips.

A nurse in lime green scrubs twisted a needle in my arm. "I need to change your IV. Hold still before you break this needle in half and we have to dig it out of your arm," she ordered.

I muttered curses under my breath while Nurse Ratchet finished torturing me. "All done, sweetheart," she said, tossing her latex gloves in the trash. "You best put on your happy face. Your friends have been here for hours, waiting for you to wake up." I turned my head. Lenny, Don and Jerome stood beside my hospital bed like sentinels.

"*Baruch Ha'Shem*, she's awake!" Lenny exclaimed. "I've been praying for you, and so has Rabbi Goldberg."

Goldberg! At the sound of his name, my jaw tightened. How could Lenny still be hanging around with the man behind my attempted assassination? Before I could ruminate any further, Don kissed my forehead. "Janey, you're going to be OK. I promise I will personally arrest the bastard that did this to you."

"I know where to find him," I croaked.

Don held his finger to his lips, shussing me. "We'll talk about it when you get out of the hospital. "Don!" I protested, but he was on his cell phone, not listening to me. Jerome lowered his peroxide blond head to my level. "Girlfriend, I've been worried sick over you. Woman-to-woman, let Don and the police handle this. Keep your skinny butt outta this."

I gave Jerome a pleading look. "You've got to get me out of here. I need to hunt down the killer. Please help me."

"There's nothing I can do," Jerome said. "The doctor says you need to rest up in the hospital." I gave Jerome the finger then passed out.

The clock on my night table read two am. I pulled the sheet over my head to shield my eyes from the relentless glare of the fluorescent lights. It was no use, more light spilled in from the hallway. Nurses and orderlies clattered down the hallway pushing oversized medical carts laden with equipment. Machines beeped like R2D2. Scratchy speakers called nurses to their stations at thirty second intervals. I pictured Don fast asleep in our king sized bed with a Baltimore Ravens quilt tucked under his stubbly chin, Archie and Eve snuggled against his warm body.

Jesus, I was a mess. I was, all alone, half-deaf and recovering from gunshot wounds in an inner city hospital. I licked my parched lips. A metallic taste filled my mouth and my nose twitched from the odor of antiseptic chemicals. Plastic IV bags hung next to my bed, streaming a powerful cocktail of drugs into my engorged veins, a nasal cannula circulated oxygen into my damaged lung. My left arm was at a forty-five degree angle in sling. I touched the large cottony bandage covering my left ear.

My good ear detected a suspicious sound in the hallway that set my nervous system on high alert. Had Yuri snuck in to the hospital to finish me off? I tried to stand up, forgetting that my arm was in a sling and that I had a needle implanted in my arm. Pain spilled down the right side of my body like acid. I collapsed back down on the narrow bed. More strange sounds, closer this time. I need a weapon. From my uneaten dinner tray I grabbed a plastic knife it. "Who's there?" I cried out, gripping the flimsy blade.

A woman's head peeped around the doorway. I recognized the wig. Rabbi Goldberg's wife Shayna strode into the room carrying a shopping bag from the Star K Super Kosher Market.

"You scared the crap out of me!" I said, dropping the knife. "What the hell are you doing here in the middle of the night?"

"I thought you'd need some homemade chicken soup with matzo balls," she said innocently, taking a steaming container out of the bag and pouring it into a bowl. She pushed the bowl toward me, "They don't call it Jewish penicillin for nothing, *essen,* eat."

"Thanks," I said, slurping the velvety broth. I hadn't eaten anything in more than twenty-four hours, my stomach felt like a

Dog Spelled Backwards

bottomless pit. I polished off the bowl then held it out for more.

Shayna plopped a grapefruit-size matzo ball into the broth. She watched me eat, nervously tapping her finger nails on my bedrail.

"I have a confession," she said. "I didn't come here just to deliver chicken soup." I held out the bowl for a third helping. Shayna adjusted her *sheitel* and smoothed her long skirt.

"I haven't been completely honest with you," Shayna said.

I squinted at her. "What the hell does that mean?"

Shayna lowered her eyes as she spoke. "I was just seventeen when I married Avram. Like most Orthodox marriages, it was arranged. I didn't have any say in the matter, but I wanted to please my parents and live a righteous life. Avram came from a good family. He was studying in *yeshiva* to be a rabbi; a noble man, I thought, every Orthodox Jewish woman's dream.

After our first son was born Avram started staying out late, coming home at all hours stinking of alcohol. There were phone calls in the middle of the night, people with strange accents. When I asked Avram about it he said, 'shut up or I'll punch you in the mouth.'

One night I went through his coat. I found ten thousand dollars and stacks of betting slips. All that money and he only gave me twenty dollars a week for food! I put the money back and didn't say anything."

Shayna paused, dabbing tears from her eyes. "Avram was constantly traveling to Atlantic City, Las Vegas, Brooklyn. I was sure he was gambling and, God forbid, laundering money—or worse. Why else would he always have so much cash around the house? When Yuri came to our house I knew Avram was a criminal. Yuri never said a word to me, he cocked his finger at me like he had a gun. I was petrified of him. The last straw was when our oldest daughter was playing one *shabbos* in Avram's office. She ran into the kitchen

Dog Spelled Backwards

with a gun in her tiny hand yelling 'Mommy, mommy, look what daddy has in his desk!' After that, I watched Avram like a hawk. I took down every phone number, wrote down the license plate numbers of the men who came to see him. I even took pictures." Shayna's face momentarily brightened and she laughed heartily. "You think you're the only one who knows how to spy? I've read all of Laura Lippman's books. Tess Monaghan is my hero."

"Tess, who?" I said.

Shayna sighed. "I knew you'd never suspect that I could do anything except shop for wigs, make babies and go to synagogue. When Avram hired you to gather information on Rabbi Dworkin, I feared for your life. I was so worried that I sent Pinchas to follow your car." My mind flashed back to the skinny kid I met at Rabbi Goldberg's house, the first to warn me to watch my back. He must have been the one tailing my car, maybe even the mystery man who followed me to Rabbi Goldberg's house.

Shayna continued. "Everyone in the Orthodox community knows about Rabbi Dworkin's black market kidneys. They tolerate him because they believe he is performing a public service, even if what he charges bankrupts them. I knew Avram wanted the kidney business all to himself. And that means killing Dworkin." She looked me squarely in the eye. "And killing you, too."

A screeching alarm sounded to warn that my IV bags were empty and a nurse was on her way. "Talk fast Shayna," I warned. "Why didn't you leave when he first threatened you?"

"It's not that easy," Shayna said, gathering her things. "I had no money, four young children, and no place to go. Besides, Avram would never grant me a Jewish divorce. I'd be forced to leave my community and live among strangers."

I felt a pang of sympathy for Shayna. I'd been homeless and penniless before. Shayna had opted to stay and fight. I admired that. I'd totally underestimated Shayna, seeing her only as a cookie cutter

Dog Spelled Backwards

Orthodox Jewish housewife under her husband's thumb, incapable of independent thought and action.

"I have a proposition," Shayna said. "I can help you put Avram and Yuri in prison," Shayna said.

"How?"

Shayna gave me a conspiratorial wink. "I put a surveillance camera in Avram's office. The tapes show Avram giving Yuri orders to kill you and Rabbi Dworkin and Yuri giving Avram stacks of money in exchange for a box of AK-47 rifles. It makes me sick to my stomach know my husband is a... *scumbag*." Shayna covered her mouth as if she'd just eaten some rotten meat.

I didn't have the heart to tell her that her video tapes might not hold up in court. But that was beside the point. I was only too happy to help Shayna nail these two.

"You have my respect Shayna. You're a tough chick, that's my highest compliment."

Shayna smiled. "We're both tough Jewish women. It's written in Proverbs: *A woman of valor, who can find her? Her price is far above rubies."*

"Amen to that," I said, high fiving Shayna with my uninjured arm. "Now get me out of this stinking hospital so we can kick some ass."

18 Welcome to the Jungle

The following night Don came to see me. He was dressed in his Baltimore City police uniform, his heavy utility belt slung low against his hips like a cowboy ready for a gunfight. His face was freshly shaven and his uniform was clean and pressed.

"You look a shade better than death warmed over," he said, holding my hand. He jerked this thumb to my dinner tray. "You're eating. That's always a good sign."

I'd scarfed down the hospital's blue plate special of leathery meat loaf and half-cooked mashed potatoes smothered with lumpy gravy. As repulsive as the food was, I'd need every last calorie to fuel myself for this evening's show down with Rabbi Goldberg.

"I know how much you miss Archie," Don continued. "So I brought you this little guy to keep you company." He handed me a stuffed toy poodle. "I tried to get a bull terrier but Target was all out," he said apologetically.

"Thanks Don," I said, motioning him closer so I could give him a peck on the cheek. "I promise to behave myself and follow my doctor's orders." Don was a good guy. All he wanted was for me to get better and to love him back. Why was it so hard for me to do that?

Don cocked his head to one side, the same look Archie gave me when he was was worried that I'd run out of kibble. I was certain Don knew I was lying through my teeth, but better to ask for forgiveness than to beg for permission.

"I'll stop by in the morning after I get off my shift," Don said, squeezing my hand. "And I'll bring you a pizza from Matthew's for breakfast."

Dog Spelled Backwards

I licked my lips. "Pizza for breakfast. You're the best, Don," I said, already tasting the gooey mozzarella cheese. "Be safe out there," I said. "Think of me when you're arresting some perps."

Don gave the stuffed dog a pat on the head. "Will do, ma'am," he said walking out of the room. The second Don was out of earshot I dialed Shayna's cell phone. "It's go time," I said. "Get your ass over here."

Forty minutes later, Shayna was in my room holding two shopping bags. "More chicken soup?" I said hopefully. "Sorry, not this time," she said. "But I've got some clean clothing for you. I figured you wouldn't want to put on your blood-stained shirt and jeans." Shayna held up a dark blue dress and a long-sleeved, white button down shirt. I rolled my eyes. I thought I'd never have to put on these damn frumpy clothes again. "I know how much you hate this," Shayna said, loading my dirty clothing into the shopping bags. "But I didn't have any of your style of clothing at my house."

I sighed. "Whatever, Shayna. I'll live—as long as this is the last time I've gotta dress like a nun."

Shayna wheeled over the medicine cart the nurse left in my room. I looked at the IV line in my arm and raised an eyebrow. "I know how to do this," Shayna said, expertly withdrawing the needle from my vein. She swabbed the reddened area with alcohol then bandaged my arm. "How do you know how to do this?" I asked as Shayna turned off my monitors and shut down my supplemental oxygen. She sat me up in bed. "I spent two years studying nursing at the University of Maryland," she said in a matter-of-fact voice. "Avram forced me to quit. He said I needed to stay home with the children and stop associating with non-Jews."

Shayna lowered my bed then pushed the medicine cart aside. Painfully, I eased my broken body out of bed and shakily stood up. The room spun like a carnival ride. I gripped the side rail for balance and fought back the urge to puke on Shayna. "Easy," Shayna said cooly. "I've got something that to help you." Before I could say "what the

Dog Spelled Backwards

hell?" Shayna jabbed my arm with a syringe. "Zofran, an anti-emetic," she said. "It'll shut down the nausea. You should be good to go in fifteen minutes."

I eyed Shayna's purse warily. "What else have you got in your bag of tricks?" She shot me a shit-eating grin. "I've got a big surprise for you," she said, digging into her satchel and pulling an object out of her bag.

I gasped. "I believe you dropped this little item on my front lawn." She held my taser by its butt like she was handling a dead animal.

"Get that back in your purse," I ordered. The last I needed was for Shayna to do anything stupid, like zap a doctor or accidentally taser herself. "Relax. No one ever suspects an Orthodox woman," Shayna giggled. "How do you think I managed to walk in and out of this place after hours."

In a flash, I was cleaned up and dressed in the clothes Shayna brought for me. The Zofran had kicked in and I was feeling slightly less nauseated. "Ready to roll," I said. Shayna gently slung my black leather motorcycle jacket over my shoulders to camouflage my wounded left arm. I sighed, noting the bullet holes that had pierced my favorite jacket.

"Perfect," Shayna said, tying a blue and yellow kerchief over my head to hide my bandaged ear. I insisted on wearing my Doc Marten boots rather than the battered clogs Shayna tried to force onto my feet. "I probably look like a mash up of punk meets pious," I joked. Shayna looked at me blankly.

No one gave us a second look as we left my hospital room. All the nurses were busy tending to patients. Shayna and I took the elevator down to the hospital's main floor. We needed to walk through the emergency room to get to Shayna's mini van.

The elevator doors shuddered open, revealing a chaotic room filled with men, women and wailing children all crowding around a reception desk staffed by a lone nurse. My God, I thought, Baltimore's own Night of the Living Dead.

The line to see the beleaguered nurse snaked around the airless room. Near the back wall, two security guards stood next to a candy machine checking their phones. It would probably take a nuclear bomb to go off before these two would look up from their texting. A woman leaned against a pillar, violently sobbing into a blood-soaked towel, her young son hugging her filthy pant leg. Two men pounded their fists against the door of the men's room then started kicking it, cursing at the top of their lungs in a language I didn't understand.

"Wait your damn turn," an old man growled at a teen-age boy who cut in front of him. "Shut up, motherfucker," the kid sassed back. The old man whacked the kid squarely across his face with his cane. "Respect your elders 'else I'm gonna smack you again. Hear?" Shayna steered me by my good arm past the old man who was ready to give the teenager another crack with his cane. "Settle down pops," I said as I sidled by.

I stood on the cracked sidewalk outside the emergency room counting the ambulances, taxis and cars as they zoomed up to the entrance way. A Baltimore City police car nearly crashed into one of the ambulances. Two angry cops yanked a naked, handcuffed man out of the back of the squad car and frog marched him past me. "Move!" the cops ordered. I jumped out of way so the naked man's dick wouldn't touch me.

Seconds later, a fleet of paramedics tumbled out of the back of an ambulance. "Get a crash cart. We've got a code blue cardiac on the bus," the lead paramedic shouted to a nurse smoking a cigarette by an overflowing ashtray. The nurse frowned and flicked the cigarette into the gutter. She turned on her heel and sauntered back into the maw.

By the time Shayna held the passenger door open for me, I'd grown bored of the sheer volume of human carnage.

Shayna moved juice boxes and kid's books off the seat and bid me to sit down. "A little bit different from Westwood, huh Shayna?" I teased. Shayna bit her lip and gripped the steering wheel. Before she could object, I turned the car radio to a classic rock station and thumbed the volume to high.

The mini van cabin vibrated as Axel Rose shrieked, *"Welcome to the jungle, we take it day by day, If you want it you're gonna bleed but it's the price to pay,"* from the cheap speakers. I hit the button to make the song even louder. Shayna whacked my hand away. "Turn that insanity off," Shayna scolded.

"If only I could," I said flatly. "Get used to it."

19 Thelma and Louise

We rode in silence, driving past the decrepit mini mall under the Jones Falls Expressway that housed Big Boyz Bail Bonds. I wondered if Jerome was working late writing bonds for gangster wanna-bes, or if he was unwinding at Club Charles, getting sloshed on wine coolers and gossiping with his fellow drag queens. He'd be worried once he found out that I'd escaped from the hospital. But I couldn't tell anyone, not even Jerome, what Shayna and I were up to.

With my system pumped full of morphine, I forget how badly I'd been wounded, about bullet hole in my shoulder,

Dog Spelled Backwards

my punctured lung, and the half of my ear blown to smithereens. But now that the morphine was wearing off my head felt like someone was doing home renovations on my skull and my shoulder burned like it had been branded.

"Did you to grab some Percocet from the hospital?" I asked Shayna. She kept her eyes on the expressway and her foot on the accelerator. I eyed the speedometer, we were doing eighty-five miles per hour.

"There might be some aspirin in the glove box," she said.

I flipped open the glove box, found a bottle of Excedrin, and swallowed a half dozen pills. I had to get my mind off the pain.

"Are you sure you don't have any Percocet?" I pleaded. Shayna sighed. "There's a bottle in my purse. Help yourself."

I rummaged through her purse until I found the pills. My head was about to cleave in two from the pain. I gulped three Percocet, hoping they'd act fast.

Now that I was out of the hospital, I wondered what was next. I turned toward Shayna.

"You got a plan or were you going to wing this? I don't want to play Thelma to your Louise. That movie doesn't end happy."

"I have a plan," she snapped. "A fool-proof plan."

"OK Nancy Drew, how we going to handle it?"

Shayna half-turned toward me and smiled. "In spite of your *mishegas*, your craziness, I like you. You're tough, you do what you want and don't care if people like you or not. All my friends are Orthodox Jews. But for you I'll make an exception. We are friends, right?"

Friends? I'd never had women friends, but if friendship meant breaking out of a hospital and planning revenge on an evil husband and a murderous mobster, I was all for it.

"Yeah, we're best friends. Now tell me your damn plan before I change my mind."

"I bought myself a taser," Shayna said proudly. "The nice man at the gun store sold me a Stun Master 4.5 million volt Hot Shot." She jerked her head toward the back seat. "It's in that black bag."

"You went to a gun store?"

Shayna chuckled. "That's not the only thing in my bag of tricks. I grabbed two of Avram's guns. Look in the bag. Take your pick."

I flipped on the van's overhead light so I could get a better look at Shayna's cache. At the bottom of the bag sat a Glock .22 pistol, a police-issue Sig Sauer P229 and half a dozen boxes of ammunition.

I picked up the stun gun and whistled through my teeth. "Are you friggin' nuts? With all this chrome, we could get our asses thrown in prison."

Shayna wasn't listening, she was talking in a kind of trance, seduced by her insane plan and emboldened by the guns. I could see there was no reasoning with her. It was best to hear her out and pretend to go along with her plan. I pocketed the stun gun as Shayna continued babbling.

"I overheard Avram's plan. Yuri's meeting him at our house at midnight to deliver guns and get kidney money." I nodded my head for Shayna to keep talking.

"We'll surprise them in the middle of their deal. Yuri won't suspect that I have a gun, so I'll pull my pistol first. If he makes a move, taser his ass! Then we'll grab the cash and split it fifty-fifty. Yuri will think that Avram planned this whole heist as a set up. It's a genius plan, don't you think?"

My jaw hung open. "That's your plan! It's flimsier than wet toilet paper. A million things can go wrong. Can you even handle a gun?"

Shayna shot me an exasperated look. "Of course I can shoot," she snorted. "I'm a card carrying member of the NRA and I've been to the indoor gun range in White Marsh. All of the Orthodox go there."

I was having a hard time picturing Shayna as a gun moll.

"What do you propose to do with Yuri's guns, Miss Trigger Happy?" I asked.

"That's where you come in. I figured that with your, um, lifestyle, you'd know how to sell guns so we can get more money."

"My fiancee is a Baltimore City police officer. He might have a problem with me trafficking in illegal firearms."

"A minor detail," Shayna countered. "Your boyfriend has a bigger problem. His wife-to-be is in my husband's crosshairs."

"Simmer down," I said. Shayna's plan was a ridiculous, half-baked operation, something an idle housewife would cook up. But I didn't have a better plan. Someone was going to get shot. I prayed it wouldn't be me."

"Fine," I huffed. "We'll try it your way. But I'm warning you, things are going to get fucked up fast. And whatever you do, don't pull the trigger unless you absolutely have to."

"I have no problem with that." Shayna said steadily. "Please load the guns. We're almost in Westwood."

20 Breaking Bad

Shayna hit every pot hole between Baltimore and Westwood. I tried to load the Glock's magazine, but the bullets spilled onto Shayna's lap and over the front seat.

"Slow down," I yelled. "Or I'll never get the gun loaded."

Shayna squealed the brakes just as I palmed the loaded magazine into the gun. I slammed hard against the dashboard.

"God damn it!" I shouted. "The gun could have gone off."

Shayna turned to me. "Sorry, my foot slipped. I'll pull over while you lock and load."

I shook my head. "Lock and load? Who do you think you are, Sarah Palin? Where did you come up with this bullshit?"

I focused my attention back on the Glock. Shayna eyed the gun like she couldn't wait to start shooting every living thing in sight. Her manic look unnerved me. Could I trust her to safely handle a gun? A though bubbled in my brain. Maybe it was the Percocet distorting my judgement, or maybe, I'd finally figured out why Shayna got under my skin: Shayna was like me; she was a living, breathing version of my own id. Now I had to make sure my id didn't plug me in my other shoulder.

"Listen up," I said, holding the gun out of her reach. "These are Jane's gun safety rules and they will be obeyed. One: assume the gun is loaded. Two: point the gun in a safe directions. Three: keep off the trigger until you're ready to shoot. Understood?"

"Ten-four. Roger that."

"Stop talking like an idiot!"

Shayna started the mini van. We drove past Northwest High School, turned left and right through the narrow streets, then parked a block from Shayna's house. I took the taser out of the bag and warily handed it to her. "I don't trust you with a gun," I said. "I'm not even sure I want you to have this."

Shayna grabbed the taser out of my hands and pointed it at me.

"Do not point that at me!" I yelled. I was glad I didn't give Shayna the Glock. Even giving her the taser was risky.

"You've got one shot," I said watching Shayna like a hawk. "Aim for the center of the body. Two barbs will shoot out. The target will drop for sixty seconds—max. If you miss, pull the trigger against their neck and use the stun gun feature."

Shayna nodded and smiled. "I won't miss."

"You miss and we're both screwed." I put the Glock into my pocket. When Shayna wasn't looking I stuffed the Sig Sauer into my other pocket, just in case.

Shayna's house came into view as we rounded the corner. I kept my good hand on the Glock. My head was still fuzzy from the pain killers and my body weak from hunger. I wished I'd texted Jerome in case I needed extra backup. Shayna's plan was insane, but maybe, just maybe, we could pull it off.

A hundred yards from the house, I froze. The red point of a cigarette glowed in the darkness.

"Who the hell is that?" I said.

"Relax, it's Pinchas, he's on our side," said Shayna. "We need an inside person. You can trust him."

The dark figure stood up and stubbed out his cigarette.

"Give him the other gun," said Shayna. "I saw you put it in your pocket. Pinchas must be armed."

Did Shayna have eyes in the back of her head? How did she see me stash the other gun? I raised an eyebrow and handed the gun to Pinchas. "You know how to handle a Glock?" Pinchas spun it around his fore-finger like a gunslinger.

"Great," I muttered. "Another fucking cowboy."

We walked into the house single file, Shayna in the lead with me on her heels.

"Are your kids in the house?" I whispered.

"They're at my sister's house," Shayna whispered back as we tip toed down the hallway toward Rabbi Goldberg's office. With our guns drawn, we huddled outside the door. I heard someone talking and stiffened at Yuri's muffled voice.

"I bring you money, you give me guns," Yuri said.

I heard the sound of something heavy hitting metal, probably a load of guns. Rabbi Goldberg spoke. "Here's fifty grand. If you don't trust me count it."

"Is OK," Yuri chuffed. "Now we drink vodka—*na zdorovie!*"

I glanced at Shayna and Pinchas. "I'll count to three, then kick the door open. Don't fire unless fired on. Got it?"

On three, Shayna charged in first gripping the taser in both hands. Yuri wheeled around, his vodka bottle crashed to the floor.

Shayna pulled the taser's trigger. The darts shot out like mini missiles, penetrating Yuri's eyes dead center. He dropped to his knees and cursed in Russian. The taser's voltage made his eyelids whir like pinwheels. His eyes bled like squashed ripe tomatoes.

"Good shot, girlfriend," I said to Shayna. She ignored me and sprinted toward Yuri. She shoved the taser into his beefy neck and pulled the trigger. Yuri's enormous body jerked as the crackle of voltage pulsed deeper into his electrified nervous system. He lay on his side jitterbugging his arms and legs like he having a grand mal seizure. I kicked him hard in the kidney to snap him out of it. He grunted, then passed out.

I spun around, aiming the Glock at Goldberg. He sat still with his hands gripping the sides of his office chair. Pichas stood in front of him, the Sig Sauer pointed at Goldberg's heart. A stack of money the size of a laundry basket sat on the desk near a pile of handguns.

"Take it, Shayna" Goldberg pleaded, nodding his head toward the money. "The fifty thousand is all yours. Just let me go. I promise you a divorce. You'll never see me again. I swear on my mother's grave."

Shayna crossed her arms. "It's not about money, Avram. It's about living like a proper Jew. You're a disgrace to everything our religion stands for. Yes, you'll grant me divorce. Yes, I'm taking the money. And yes, I'm taking the children too!"

"I'm sorry," whined Goldberg. Tears streamed down his cheeks and his nose ran. Goldberg reached for Shayna's hand. She slapped it away.

"Shayna, dear Shanya," he blubbered. "Can we start over? Get out of Baltimore. I have family in Brazil. I'm sorry, so sorry..."

"Sorry is not in my vocabulary," Shayna sniffed. "But I'll show you mercy." She pointed to me. "Put five thousand dollars in his pocket. His passport is in the top desk drawer. Put that in too."

Dog Spelled Backwards

I dutifully stuffed the passport and money into Goldberg's coat pocket. Shayna walked over and kissed her husband's forehead.

"Get a one-way ticket to Brazil," she said softly. "And go with God."

Pinchas pulled a roll of duct tape out of his backpack and bound Goldberg's hands behind his back.

"Ouch, that's too tight," he yelped.

Pinchas snorted in disgust. Goldberg turned to me. "I'm sorry I got you into this. Please talk sense to my wife."

I shot Goldberg a dirty look and shrugged. "You married her, Goldberg. You deal with her."

I cut my eyes at Rabbi Goldberg. "You're a pussy. Men like you are all talk until the going gets rough. Then you cry like babies. And you call women the weaker sex. Ha!"

"Pinchas will take you to the airport to make sure you get on that plane," said Shayna. "And don't worry about Yuri. I'll deal with your stupid Russian."

Pinchas pulled Goldberg to his feet and frog marched him out the door. Shayna couldn't stop smiling. She rubbed her hands together like a little kid. Her stupid plan had worked. No one had gotten killed, Goldberg was out of the picture, and when Yuri disappeared, all our problems would be over.

I set the Glock on the desk and high fived Shayna. Just as our palms met, Yuri gripped my ankle with the speed of a boa constrictor squeezing its prey, yanking my body and dropping me onto my stomach. My jaw thudded into the wood floor. Yuri pulled me toward him as I fought for purchase. My good arm shot out. I grasped the leg of Goldberg's desk.

"Shayna!" I screamed.

Shayna grabbed the Glock, flew to my side, and stomped her heel onto Yuri's wrist. The bone cracked like a shot. Yuri released his grip and wailed. I skittered away, spitting out a broken tooth.

"Son of a bitch!" I cursed.

Dog Spelled Backwards

Yuri's eyes were puffed shut. Dried blood crusted his face. One of the taser darts hung from his eyelid. He huddled a corner. Shayna put the Glock to Yuri's temple and unlocked the safety. Her finger touched the trigger.

I launched forward and collided against Shayna. I wrestled the Glock out of her hand, but not before a bullet ricocheted off the desk, shooting through the pile of bills. Fragments of money floated through the air like green feathers.

"You are one crazy motherfucker, Shayna!"

I struggled to my feet and retrieved the Glock. "Do you want a dead body on your hands? Go tie him up."

Shayna bound Yuri's arms and ankles with duct tape then slapped a piece over his mouth.

"All finished," she said, pointing to Yuri who whimpered for his life. She plucked the taser dart from his eyelid. Yuri winced and kicked his bound ankles. For a second I almost felt sorry for him. Then I remembered that he'd blown off my ear and plugged my shoulder.

I reviewed the situation. Before me was a hog-tied, half-blind Russian, fifty thousand dollars in shot up cash and six illegal weapons. My impulse was to take half of the money, stash it in a secret bank account, and leave Shayna to get rid of Yuri and the guns. Then I remembered Don warning me not to do anything illegal, to call the police and not to get myself arrested.

I was in a quandary. Should I take the money or not? The old Jane wanted that money; the new Jane wanted to toe the line. I had an angel on one shoulder and a devil on the other. So I did the only sensible thing, I compromised.

Shayna beamed as she counted the money. "There's a suitcase in the other room," she squealed, jamming fat stacks of hundred dollar bills into her purse. "You can put your share in it, along with the guns. I'll deal with Yuri."

"Nope," I said flatly. "Not gonna happen."

Shayna looked at me like I'd just drowned a kitten. "What?" she cried. "I didn't bust you out of Johns Hopkins Hospital so you could chicken out. Wait here, I'll get the suitcase."

"What part of 'no' don't you understand?" I said sharply. "You're not guilt-free Shayna Goldberg. You just blasted your husband for not being a proper Jew. Now it's time for you to behave. Drop that money now! I'm calling the police."

"It's my money!"

"*Your* money? That money's from sick people who paid for illegal kidneys. In my book that's blood money. What happened to 'thou shalt not steal?'"

Shayna looked at the money, then glanced at me. I could see her mind working double time, like Jacob wrestling with the angel. After what seemed like forever, her shoulders slumped. She dropped the wad of bills in her hand and faced me.

"You're right," said Shayna, crestfallen. I'm acting like a crazy woman. This has all been too much for me."

I sighed. I chewed my nails and jackhammered my leg. We were both seduced by the idea of taking the pile money and running—screw religion and the rule of law. But this time I was determined to do the right thing. My recalibrated moral compass was finally leading me in the right direction.

"Here's the compromise Shayna. You can have all the money, every last bill. But...."

"But what?" asked Shayna impatiently.

I shook my head. "You're going to donate all fifty thousand to the National Kidney Foundation."

Shayna pouted then nodded her head.

"When the police come, tell them that Yuri broke into your house and that you subdued him. Whatever you do, don't say that you plugged him with an illegal taser. And hide that money before the cops see it."

"Think it'll work?"

"Why not, you're persuasive."

"What about the guns?"

I texted Jerome. He arrived in minutes, tottering into the room in a skin tight, chartreuse evening gown, blond wig and stiletto heels.

"I came straight from Drag Queen Poker Night at The Hippo," he huffed. "This better be a damn emergency. I was up two hundred dollars."

Jermone glanced at Yuri. "You ladies done some job on my future ex-boyfriend," he said. "That's some kinky shit."

Shayna couldn't take her eyes off Jerome's enormous fake breasts. "I've never met a real transvestite before," she said, blushing.

Jerome stood tall. With the stiletto heels he was well over six and a half feet. "Well Miss Shayna, it's my honor to be your first ladyman. You are no longer a tranny virgin."

Shaya reached out and giggled. "Are those real breasts?" Jerome squeezed the fake breasts together and jiggled them. "Got this breastplate yesterday. These titties cost me a fortune."

"Excuse me," I interrupted, pointing toward the pile of guns.

"What's with those?" asked Jerome.

"I need you to get rid of them."

Jerome stepped back. "I've helped you out of a lot of tight spots, but ditching guns will risk my booty."

"No worries Miss Thing," I said. "There's a firearms buy-back this Saturday. Sell the guns to the Baltimore Police. That will be an easy two thousand dollars in your pocket. You can buy more fake boobs."

"Since you put it that way, I'll take the guns. Now I'll skedaddle so you can get back to your *menage a trois*."

Jerome stashed the guns into a duffle bag and pranced out of the room. I waited a few minutes then handed the phone to Shayna.

"Dial 911. Say there's a burglary in progress. Wait for the police. Don't call or text anyone. Follow the plan."

"What about you?"

"I'm going home. I'm done."

Shayna walked over to me. "I'm sorry I disrespected you."

"I'm sorry I underestimated you."

Shayna threw out her arms. "Can I give you a hug?"

I stepped back. I'd never hugged another woman other than my mother. This felt weird.

"OK, you can hug me. But not too tight. My arm is killing me."

Shayna held me tenderly. Her wig tickled my neck. "Thanks for being my friend," she said. "I will never forget you."

"Same here."

Shayna's hug felt good, and I wanted to stay in her arms and talk like best friends, like sisters. Just as I was about to say more, police sirens screamed outside, and I eased out of her arms.

"Bye Shayna," I called out. I stepped over Yuri and gave him a parting kick in the kneecap. "Hope your seeing-eye dog pees on your leg."

I stood under a lone streetlight on Reisterstown Road. The bank sign across the street read three am. I had just enough money to pay for a cab back to my condo. A car pulled up alongside me as I walked down the street. "Hey," a familiar voice called. I kept walking as the car kept pace with me.

"I had a bad feeling I'd find you in Westwood. You need to be in the hospital."

I stopped and faced Don. I prayed he wasn't going to cuff me.

"Don't ask, don't tell?" I said hopefully.

"I'm not asking, I am telling you—get in this car now!"

21 Here Comes the Bride

I spent the next week in the hospital getting checked up and having reconstructive surgery to repair my shredded ear. My doctors read me the riot act for escaping from the hospital. I pretended to be contrite, that seemed to calm them down.

The day after the operation, the nurse handed me a mirror. I admired the pink, silicon prosthesis the doctors affixed to the remains of my flesh. I was glad not to look like the bride of Frankenstein, but less pleased when the audiologist said the hearing in my ear would never return.

Every night after Don's police shift ended, he brought me pizzas with extra anchovies and my favorite greasy meat ball subs from Di Pasquale's in Highlandtown. To my immense relief, Don never asked me about my night at Rabbi Goldberg's house or why I disappeared from the hospital. Don was no dummy, he knew that I'd done something fishy, but he probably didn't suspect it involved black market kidneys and illegal guns—at least I hoped not. If Don knew anything, he kept it to himself. I was content to talk about the Ravens and enjoy my meat ball sub while Don ate pizza and guzzled grape soda.

But all the while, I worried that I'd slip up and Don would discover what I'd done. Or maybe he already knew. Don played in a touch football league with members of the Westwood police force, and they were sure to fill him in on arrests involving a hog-tied, Russian who'd been shot in the eyeballs.

With my prosthetic ear in place and the bullet wounds in my shoulder healing, Don helped me get ready to be discharged. He

Dog Spelled Backwards

neatly folded my clothes and eased me into a wheel chair. Even though I could walk, I knew better than to protest.

"Ready to rock and roll?" Don joked, pushing me down the hallway toward the hospital exit then through the hospital's cavernous parking garage. Don took me in his arms and gently placed me in the passenger seat of his pick up truck. He winked and flirted with the parking garage cashier. "Keep the change sweetheart," he said slipping the woman a twenty dollar bill. "Gotta get my lady home."

Don kissed me on the cheek. "God, I've missed you," he said nuzzling my neck. As we turned onto the expressway, Don put on a Hank Williams CD. He held my hand and warbled along to "There's a Tear in my Beer." I couldn't wait to get home, shower off the hospital smell and curl up with Don in our soft bed.

The second Don opened the condo's front door, Archie and Eve hopped off the couch and bounded toward me, jumping up and slathering my face with doggie saliva. "Missed you crazy beasts," I cooed.

Lenny stood in the kitchen blowing a noisemaker and wearing a pink paper hat. "Welcome home!" he cheered, ushering me into the kitchen. "I made a chocolate layer cake, all by myself," he beamed. I gobbled three pieces then licking frosting off my fingers.

"Cousin, you've outdone yourself," I said, reaching for a glass of milk. "Lenny's been baking cakes while you were in the hospital," Don said, patting his stomach. "I've gained five pounds tasting them all."

"Is that a crime?" I said, ticking Don. "Just do some extra crunches."

"I've got a surprise for you," Lenny said. "I'm baking your wedding cake. It's a five-tiered chocolate cake with double chocolate icing with miniature bride and groom to put on top."

The wedding. How could I forget? Now that I was out of the hospital, I couldn't put it off any longer.

"When?" I asked Don.

"A week from Sunday," he replied. "I've already put in for leave. We can get married right in our backyard then go to the beach for the honeymoon."

My head spun, I didn't know if it was from the sugar rush or Don's accelerated timetable for our nuptials. I took a gulp of cold milk and wiped my lips. All this was happening too fast.

"Can we slow things down?" I said, feeling like a cornered rat. "Doesn't it take months to plan a wedding? Who's going to marry us?"

Don smiled and handed me his credit card. "Get yourself a proper wedding dress. Just promise me it will be white. I don't want any surprises."

"What about a marriage license?" I asked, stalling.

"Everything is taken care of, babe," Don said, putting his arms around me. "It's OK to be nervous. I am too."

My stomach clenched tighter than a boxer's fist. While I was in the hospital, Don and Lenny had outfoxed me by scheming this wedding. Now I had to go along with it.

"You promise everything is going to be OK?" I pleaded.

"I do," Don said with a wink. "Yes I do."

Lenny butted in. "I want to help you pick out your dress. Let's go to Fink's Bridal at the Towson Mall."

I shrugged "You two Martha Stewarts have thought about everything. OK Lenny, let's hit the mall."

The night before the wedding, Don's police buddies picked him for his bachelor party at the Hub Cap, our favorite Mt. Jefferson dive bar. As Don stepped into a rented limo I warned him not to bring home any strippers.

While Don was doing shots of Jack Daniels and shooting pool, Lenny and I sat on the couch and watched a Terminator marathon.

At four in the morning, I was still wide awake. I went into our small backyard to smoke a cigarette. Two rows of folding chairs were placed in a semi-circle in front of a wooden arbor with a blue and white cloth stretched over the top. In between

Terminator movies, Lenny explained that this was a *huppah*, the traditional canopy under which Jewish couples stand during their wedding ceremony.

At dawn, my husband-to-be stumbled in the door stinking of beer and cigars. Once inside, he collapsed on the couch, his mouth hanging wide in between raspy snores.

As much as I loved Don, I couldn't help panicking. Was it really too late to call off the wedding? To calm my nerves, I took the dogs out for a long walk. A biting November wind stung my cheeks, scattering the last autumn leaves across the street and setting my teeth chattering. I zipped up my down jacket and pulled my woolen hat over my ears.

Archie and Eve trotted ahead of me, occasionally stopping to pee or growl at squirrels. Each time they stopped, Archie playfully licked Eve's pink ears. The dogs are like an old married couple, I mused, amazed at how they'd taken to each other so quickly. I hoped my marriage would be as easy.

Dog Spelled Backwards

I had avoided intimate relationships my whole life. My only confidant had been Lenny. Within a short year, everything had changed. First I met Don, then Shayna, my first female friend. Lenny and Archie were like bookends in my life, propping me up when I wavered. I twisted my engagement ring. It wouldn't budge past my knuckle—I took it to be a sign I was stuck with Don.

The wedding ceremony was set for high noon and my time for rumination and second thoughts was fast running out. Just before noon, I sat on my bed staring at my wedding dress, nervous as a cat getting a bath. Lenny had helped me select a simple, off-white, floor-length sheath that flattered my thin figure; no lace, no train, and no veil. Simple and functional.

I struggled to get into my wedding gown. I kept twisting the dress and stepping on the hem. I cursed as the fabric ripped and the zipper jammed. I wished I could get married in my sweat pants and T-shirt. As I yanked at the zipper here was a rap at the door.

"Go away!" I yelled.

The door opened. In walked Shayna. Before I could ask what the hell she was doing in my bedroom, she'd already hugged me.

"I figured you might need a friend today," she said, zipping up the dress and smoothing the fabric. She turned me toward the mirror. "Even with one arm you're still a beautiful *kallah*. She brushed my hair so it covered my artificial ear. Before I could object, she pulled out a make-up kit and dabbed blush on my cheeks and applied a thin layer powder blue eye shadow.

"Don't fight me," Shayna ordered. "Look how gorgeous. Look at your green eyes!" I blinked, carful not to smear the mascara. I couldn't believe how feminine I looked. Shayna was right, I did look beautiful. "Yeah, I guess I am beautiful," I said tentatively. "You're a knockout," Shayna beamed. "Wait until Don gets an eyeful."

Shayna opened a jewelry box and handed me a gold, palm-shaped object on a thin chain. "I've bought you a *hamsa*, it's a traditional amulet that protects against the evil eye. We all need protection from sin." She fastened the chain around my neck. The small opal in the *hamsa's* center sparked green and blue against my pale neck.

"It's beautiful," I said fingering the *hamsa*. "How did you know it was my wedding day?"

"Lenny called me. He said you needed some female support."

I laughed. "Lenny was so excited about my wedding he practically tried on my wedding dress. Will you stay for the ceremony?"

Shayna shook her head. "The children and I are going to California. We're going to live in Los Angeles for a fresh start. The moving truck will be here soon."

I looked away. Damn, I finally made a friend and now she was moving across the country.

"I'll miss you, Shayna. Or should I say Louise?"

"I'll miss you too, Thelma," Shayna said, hugging me tightly and kissing me on both cheeks. *"Mazel tov, Jane,"* Shayna whispered in my good ear. "May God bless you and keep you." Shayna blew me a kiss and left.

For once, Lenny didn't look like a train wreck. Instead of his usual saggy sweat pants and food-stained shirts, he wore a tailored pin stripe suit with a red rose in his lapel. Even his unruly hair was cut and styled. He looked handsome and I was proud that he was walking me down the aisle.

"Ready Jane?" Lenny said, hooking his arm in mine. I took a deep breath and began my slow walk toward the *huppa*. I nodded woodenly to the dozen guests; fellow cops from Don's squad and a trio of barflies from the Hub Cap, the dive bar where Don and I had our first date. Charlie O., one of the Hub cap regulars, let out a wolf whistle as I walked by. I shot him the finger for old time's sake.

Don stood under the *huppa* smiling nervously. His pressed gray suit, slicked back hair and dimple chin, made him look like a movie star. My heart skipped a beat at my handsome, husband-to-be.

Lenny walked me next to Don. He kissed my cheek in a fatherly way then sat down next to his fiancee.

Don and I stood together in front of the *huppa,* shivering in the November cold. I hoped the ceremony would be over quickly so I could go inside and put on something warm. Don put his arms around me and I snuggled against him.

"Thanks for taking care of all the details," I said. "But who's going to marry us?"

"Trust me, Jane. I promise you won't be disappointed."

Just then I heard a familiar voice. "Excuse *moi.* Make way, I'm coming through."

My jaw dropped as Jerome rushed to the *huppa* dressed in a black silk robe with a white satin *yarmulka.*

"*You're* marrying us?"

"Yes honey, I most certainly am. If you both agree that I am clergy, then it's all a hundred percent legal in the great state of Maryland. In honor of your late mother, this is your Jewish wedding."

Don cocked an eyebrow at me. "Do you agree?"

"I do, Don," I said squeezing his hand.

"Then unbunch your panties Miss Jane," Jerome said. "And let's get this wedding started."

22 The Honeymoon is Over

Don and I sped across the Bay Bridge on our way to Ocean City. The beach in early winter was my idea of paradise. More seagulls than people, no screaming, snot-nosed kids and miles of wind-swept beach all to ourselves. Don reserved the honeymoon suite in the Seadrift Hotel. Knowing that I'd never leave Archie and Eve behind, Don make sure the hotel took dogs, so the five of us could spent the honeymoon together as a family.

The first days were clear and cold, all blue skies and pounding surf. Don rose at the crack of dawn and ran the dogs along the hard-packed sand. By the time they got back to the room, muddy, bedraggled and happy as clams, I'd already brewed a strong pot of coffee and fried up a dozen eggs.

While Don was gone I slept late then walked with my coffee mug in hand along the beach, picking up shells then tossing them back into the roaring ocean.

It was good to be alone with my thoughts. I needed space to figure things out and most of all, to get my strength back. My life was like an old pair of clothes that I loved, but didn't fit me anymore; too tight in some places and too baggy in others. I wasn't quite ready to throw the old Jane completely under the bus, but I needed to make some changes. It was time to launch Jane Ronson version 2.0.

As the week went on, the weather worsened. Grey clouds gathered as cold rains battered the beach, even the hardy sandpipers disappeared. The dogs didn't want to go out into the rain and cold, so they stayed curled up in a furry pile on the couch. Don and I holed up in our near-deserted hotel ordering pizza, watching cable TV, and and doing our best to make up for all the sex we'd missed out on the last six months.

When I couldn't stomach another slice of Domino's triple cheese and pepperoni pizza, we snuck out of the hotel, leaving Archie and Eve snoring on the bed. Don surprised me with dinner at a five star restaurant in Rehoboth Beach. Don chatted up the waiters. He told them that it was the last night of our honeymoon.

The waiters made a big fuss over us, seating us at a beach view table and comping us a bottle of pink champagne. The champagne was cheap stuff, sweet and watery, but we didn't care.

Don held his glass aloft. "To my wife and best friend," he toasted. "Here's to our future. Nothing but blue skies ahead, babe." We clinked glasses and I resumed polishing off my bloody-rare, filet mignon and baked potato slathered in sour cream.

My belly was practically bursting when the waiter delivered the last course, an enormous slice of Smith Island Cake with an inch of dark frosting on the top. The mere smell of it nearly sent me into a chocolate coma.

"Eat up it all because this place doesn't believe in doggie bags" Don said, sawing his fork through the fifteen rich layers of creamy chocolate. I obeyed, gobbling every last crumb then licking my fork tines like a starving dog. Man, life was good.

Back at the hotel, we fed Archie and Event their kibble then went to bed. Don fell into a deep sleep while I stared at the ceiling. I lay awake listening to Don and the dogs saw wood, hoping that would lull me to sleep.

My stomach hurt from too much food and I burped up a piece of cake. I pinched the tiny roll of fat at my waist then twisted my wedding ring. When had it gotten so tight on my finger? Had I gained weight? I hadn't exercised in weeks; with my arm still in a sling and my lung mending, I couldn't walk far, much less run my customary wind sprints. I hoped my kick boxing days weren't over but my arm was still months away from me hitting the heavy bag. Besides, I'd promised Don and the doctors that I'd take it easy for the next few months. I touched the scar on my mangled left ear, tracing the rough outline with my forefinger. I snapped my fingers near my left ear to see if any hearing had returned. No luck.

My mind spun like a whirligig while my muscles twitched. I couldn't calm down. It didn't help that a nor'easter had blown in, the winds off the Atlantic Ocean rattled the sliding glass doors.

There was no use trying to force myself to sleep. I put on my clothes and tip toed out of the bedroom. I plopped two Alka-Seltzer tables in a glass then sat on the couch with my iPad open in front of me, drumming my fingers against the coffee table. Something wouldn't let me rest, and it wasn't because I'd eaten too much chocolate or slugged down too much flat champagne.

I tugged on the lobe of my artificial ear and chewed my lip. It had been almost too easy to catch Rabbi Goldberg. Things clicked into place with too much precision. The Orthodox community in Westwood

Dog Spelled Backwards

was too tightly woven for an outsider to fully penetrate; why had they let me in? I'd trusted Shayna, and at the time, was sure her motives were pure and that she was telling me the truth. Shayna wanted her husband punished for being a criminal and for betraying her trust in him as a righteous Jew. And what woman doesn't want revenge for a husband who threatens to beat the crap out of her?

I gulped down the Alka-Seltzer. I thought long and hard about the facts: Goldberg wanted Rabbi Dworkin's black market kidney operation for his own. Goldberg hired Yuri to kill me once he'd digested all the information I'd fed to him. Rabbi Dworkin and Dr. Kornblatt were gone, fled to Israel where they couldn't face extradition to the United States. The house where the kidney operations had taken place had been raided by the police, evidence collected and catalogued. And Kornblatt's patients? Had they died because they could no longer count on getting their black market kidneys, or, had they....

"Damn it!" I cried out, slamming my right hand on the table so hard I nearly knocked my iPad to the floor. I clicked on the craigslist web page. Holding my breath, I scrolled through the listings. Halfway through I saw the post I'd been dreading:

"SELL YOUR KIDNEY. DO A GOOD DEED AND EARN BIG $$$$$. EMAIL INFO@INEEDURKIDNEY.ORG."

How had I been so fucking stupid? I'd checked craigslist after Goldberg had been arrested to make sure the posting had been deleted.

Who the hell had posted this?

I typed a reply using one of my untraceable email addresses, the ones I used to use when chasing down predators.

Healthy, twenty-five-year-old. Broke. *How do I sell my kidney?*

My fingers hovered over the send button. I clicked and waited. My computer pinged seconds later.

Call me now. 443-555-2976.

I picked up the hotel phone and punched the numbers. At the other end a phone rang twice.

"Hello," woman said. "Hello, hello. Who's calling?"

"It's Jane." I hissed. "God help you Shayna."

I slammed the phone against the wall. *Shayna had played me!*

I should have suspected she was behind this scheme, waiting until I was out of the picture to take over her husband's operation.

I gritted my teeth pounded my fists. I'd missed all the clues because I wanted desperately to believe that Shayna was my friend, and that I could trust her. A thousand vengeful thoughts raced through my head. I lit a cigarette and took furious drags, exhaling the smoke from my nostrils like an enraged bull.

I could hunt Shayna down, turn her in to the police. But Shayna knew too much, she'd be sure to tell the cops about my involvement. Don would never trust me, he'd know I lied to him. Shit, I could pretend I never saw Shayna's kidney posting on craigslist, go on with my new life like nothing ever happened. Could I let this be?

"What are you doing out there?" Don called from the bedroom.

"Just going out for some fresh air," I said, trying to hide my anger. If Shayna thought she could play me, she picked the wrong girl. I grabbed my car keys and stepped out into the night.

Dog Spelled Backwards

About the Author

Jill Yesko is a journalist and NPR commentator. Her work has been published in numerous national magazines. She is the author of the acclaimed crime fiction novels *Murder in the Dog Park*, *Dog Spelled Backwards* and the forthcoming *Sleeping Dogs Don't Lie*. Before her career in journalism, Jill was a national-class cyclist and graduate student in cultural geography. When not writing, Jill patrols Baltimore's dog parks with her basset hound.

Visit Jill at

www.murderinthedogpark.com.

CPSIA information can be obtained at www.ICGtesting.com
Printed in the USA
BVOW03s1303190913

331541BV00004B/8/P